THE
HIGH
CLIMBER
OF
DARK
WATER
BAY

THE HIGH CLIMBER OF DARK WATER BAY

Caroline Arden

TURNER PUBLISHING COMPANY

Turner Publishing Company
Nashville, Tennessee
New York, New York

www.turnerpublishing.com

The High Climber of Dark Water Bay

Cover design: Maddie Cothren
Book design: Tim Holtz
Library of Congress Cataloging-in-Publication Data
Names: Arden, Caroline (Writer of young adult fiction), author.
Title: The high climber of Dark Water Bay / Caroline Arden.
Description: Nashville, Tennessee. : Turner Publishing Company, [2018] |
  Summary: Orphaned in 1929 Lizzie, twelve, is sent to a Vancouver logging camp where the camp boss, a scoundrel, gives her a perilous job while seeking ransom from her absent uncle.
Identifiers: LCCN 2018004194 | ISBN 9781683367796 (pbk. : alk. paper)
Subjects: | CYAC: Logging--Fiction. | Sex role--Fiction. | Orphans--Fiction.
  | Depressions--1929--Fiction. | Vancouver (B.C.)--History--20th century--Fiction. | Canada--History--1914-1945--Fiction.
Classification: LCC PZ7.1.A735 Hig 2018 | DDC [Fic]--dc23
LC record available at https://lccn.loc.gov/2018004194

9781683367796

Printed in the United States of America
18 19 20 21   10 9 8 7 6 5 4 3 2 1

To Owen

THE
HIGH
CLIMBER
OF
DARK
WATER
BAY

CHAPTER ONE

On a mild June evening, Lizzie Parker watched three classmates climb over a wall. Sixth grade had ended the week before, and the girls were sneaking onto the school's play yard. Not that they were particularly sly. Lizzie and her best friend Mary could hear the laughter from a block away.

"They're asking for trouble," said Mary, frowning.

Lizzie watched as the last girl jumped off the wall into the play yard, her hair lifting in the breeze, her skirt flouncing as she shrieked. Part of Lizzie wanted to tell Mary to lighten up. It looked fun to leap off a wall. But another part understood that she, just as much as Mary, was not that type of girl. She and Mary were plain girls. Plain brown hair, plain brown shoes, plain checked dresses. They did plain things, such as looking at magazines at the pharmacy and walking home in time for supper, which is what they had done that afternoon.

Lizzie and Mary continued down North Green Lake Way. Seattle days were long, now that it was summer. It was nearly six-thirty, but the sun was still warm. Two men smoked and chatted on the sidewalk. A woman hurried along with groceries. A streetcar rumbled past.

"Didn't Thomas have a job interview today?" Mary asked.

Now Lizzie felt guilty for thinking Mary was no fun. Mary always asked the right questions. She was her best friend since kindergarten.

"Yes, but who knows if he got it."

"Well, if it's not this one, then he'll get another one. You just can't go to Portland." Portland. Last week after supper, Lizzie's sister, Esther, had announced that unless Thomas, Esther's husband, found work soon, Lizzie would have to live with his aunt in Portland come September. Lizzie had never met Thomas's aunt. Lizzie had known there wasn't a lot of money, but she hadn't understood just how little. Little enough that you have to send your own sister away.

"And Esther wants to take in boarders?" asked Mary. "Like a hotel?"

"Yes, but a small one. They'd put cots in the parlor."

"I can't imagine having strangers in the house."

"But they'd pay two dollars a week. I don't pay anything."

"You shouldn't have to. It's your home!"

"Well, sort of."

Lizzie heard the sadness in her own voice. Her home—her real home—was where she had grown up, where she had lived with her father. But he had died the year before, and that home was gone.

"I'm sorry," said Mary softly. "You're right. That's not what I meant. But at least Seattle is your home, not

Portland. So tell Thomas to find a job just as quick as he can."

"I will." Lizzie tried to make her voice cheerful even though she was filled with worry. Seattle *was* her home. She and Mary were supposed to start seventh grade at Lewis and Clark School on Forty-first Street. Lizzie's nephew, Robert, was going to learn to walk any day now, and Esther was going to have a new baby in the fall. Seattle was where she belonged.

The girls reached the corner where Mary turned to walk to her house.

"I've got my fingers crossed for Thomas's job," said Mary. She held up her fingers, then gave Lizzie a tight hug.

Alone, Lizzie walked slowly. She was in no rush to return to Esther's house. Thomas had likely not gotten the job. He'd been looking for months, and it was always bad news. He'd worked before at a shipyard doing some kind of engineering, but that shipyard, along with many of the others, had shut down.

It was the Depression, said Lizzie's civics teacher, Mr. Samson. There had been a stock market crash, and now people had less money. A lot less. Not that Mr. Samson had to tell Lizzie. The crash had killed her father.

When she thought about his death, it came to her in one image. It was late at night. She should have been in bed, but she had gone downstairs for a glass of water. There he had been, sitting at the long oval table in their dining room. His collar was undone, his hair was out of place, and his eyes were pink and swollen. In front of him was a stack of papers. Looking back on it, she understood they had been bills. Bills he couldn't pay because his money had been lost in the crash.

"I'm sorry," her father had said. Not to her but to a corner of the room. He hadn't looked at her. He hadn't asked why she was awake or what she needed. "I'm sorry," he'd said, again and again.

The next memory wasn't something she'd seen but something she had heard. She'd eavesdropped from the hall outside the parlor. Mr. Underhill, her father's law partner, had told Esther their father had died. "I found him this morning on the couch in his office. He took too many pills to sleep. It must've been an accident."

"He doesn't do things by accident," Esther had said.

Which meant he had taken them on purpose.

No one said suicide. No one at the memorial service, no one at school, no one in the neighborhood. Even Lizzie, now, on a warm summer evening, climbing the stairs to her sister's house, almost didn't hear the word in her own mind.

"You're late," said Esther. She was at the kitchen counter arranging thin slices of potato into a casserole dish. She wore a smock-style dress with a rose pattern so faded it was barely visible, a hand-me-down from their neighbor. Thomas's brown leather slippers slid around her feet. She was six months pregnant, and her feet were too swollen to squeeze into her regular shoes.

One-year-old Robert squawked from his high chair.

4

"Will you feed him?" asked Esther. Her blond hair was unraveling from its bun, and sweat beaded on her forehead. She unscrewed a jar of rice cereal, and Robert began to smack his lips and wave his arms.

"Hello, my peach," said Lizzie, sitting down next to him. He did look like a peach. His thin layer of hair was golden-orange, and his cheeks were plump and pink. For Christmas, she'd knit him a pair of green soakers to go over his diapers. Felt leaves decorated the back. The soakers had long since grown snug, and she'd started new ones. Yellow, so they'd suit a baby girl if that's what came next.

Robert slurped his cereal. Esther shut the casserole into the oven and began wiping potato peels into the rubbish bin. She worked quickly and did not land a single peel on the floor. Esther and Lizzie's mother had died when Lizzie was a baby and Esther was ten. Because of the difference in age, Esther had always acted like a stand-in mother, even before their father died. For instance, Esther was the reason Lizzie wore her hair in braided pigtails even though most of the other girls in her class, including Mary, had bob haircuts. "Too much effort," said Esther. "You'd need a haircut every month. And all to pretend to be some movie star."

Lizzie wore dresses from the clearance section of the Sears Roebuck catalog. Today was a drop-waist sailor dress with pink checks. In the back, the fabric, flimsy to start with, was so threadbare that she knew it'd split any day. Perhaps before school started again, there would be money for a new dress.

"Is Thomas home yet?" asked Lizzie.

"Not yet. He was supposed to be home from the interview half an hour ago."

"Maybe that's a good sign."

"Maybe." Esther heaved Robert up out of his high chair. She sniffed his diaper and turned to Lizzie. "Will you tend the pork chops while I change him?"

Esther handed Lizzie a spatula and carried Robert to the bedroom. Only three pieces of meat were in the pan. In the winter Esther would have bought enough for seconds, but not now. Lizzie lifted a corner of one chop with her spatula. The meat looked the correct shade of brown, so she flipped it over. As she lifted the third, a pop of hot oil spattered onto her finger.

"Ouch!" She flinched and flicked the chop onto the stovetop, and the spatula clattered to the floor. She tried to lift the chop with her thumb and forefinger, but it was too hot. She found an oven mitt and plopped the meat back into the pan. She took the spatula to the sink to rinse it.

Then, a smell of burning. She looked to the stove and saw flames. The oven mitt!

"Esther!" shouted Lizzie.

By the time Esther came back, holding Robert, Lizzie was holding a pot of water over the flames, about to pour.

"Stop!" yelled Esther. "What are you doing?"

She snatched the pot from Lizzie and turned off the gas. Then she dumped out the water into the sink and put the pot upside-down over the flames.

"Never put water on a fire like that! You will just make it worse. You need to smother it, don't you know that? And why was the mitt on fire?"

"I left it there," admitted Lizzie in a small voice. Tears welled in her eyes, and she felt her chin crumpling.

"Did you take the meat off the stove?"

Lizzie shook her head.

"What is wrong with you?" asked Esther, her eyes bright with anger. She squeezed Robert into his chair, dumped the charred meat into the rubbish bin, and then checked under the pot. The mitt was still smoldering. The chops were ruined. "And now what are we going to have for dinner? That meat cost twenty cents."

Robert, who had been wide-eyed but silent, began to wail. Lizzie picked him up from his chair, bounced him on her knee, and shushed him. His sobs made her want to sob too.

What *was* wrong with her? Twenty cents, gone, and all her fault.

"I'm sorry," she said.

Esther rummaged through cans in the cupboard and kept her back turned. "When I was ten and mother was dying, I could cook an entire dinner by myself. Father spoiled you with those housekeepers. Now you can't do anything."

Can't do anything. Lizzie's eyes started to well with tears again, but she held them back. After her father had died, she'd learned how: look at something, anything, small and unimportant, and then skim along the surface of things.

She fixed her eyes on a place at the edge of Robert's high chair where paint had chipped off, but she didn't go deep into seeing it. She made her breath shallow, in her throat, until it felt like she was breathing without moving. She tensed her shoulders tight around her until her whole body was stiff. She didn't want Portland, or pork chops, or Esther. Please let it all go away.

"Everything all right?" It was Thomas. He entered the kitchen and sniffed the air.

"Just a little pork chop fire," said Esther lightly, kissing her husband on the cheek. "We'll be having chipped beef."

"Grand," he said, joining Lizzie and Robert at the table. "And how's this little pipsqueak?" He stroked the baby on his cheek. Thomas was five years older than Esther, and tonight he looked even older. Gray gathered in the dark hair at his temples. Wrinkles made the skin around his eyes look delicate, like tissue paper.

"How was the interview?" asked Esther. Her voice was light, but Lizzie could hear the tension in it.

"No luck. Over a hundred fellas applied for one lousy job as a shop hand. Then the streetcar broke down. That's why I'm late."

Esther reassured Thomas that he'd find something else, and Lizzie tried to smile. She tried not to think or feel anything. She was headed to Portland, and there was nothing to do about it.

Lizzie set the table while Thomas read the paper and Esther put Robert to sleep. Then the three of them ate chipped beef and potato casserole in gloomy silence.

At the end of the meal, Thomas looked to Esther. She gave him a little nod. To Lizzie, he said, "There's something we ought to tell you."

"About Portland?"

"No. Something else." His voice was always gentle, but tonight there was something worrisome about the gentleness. "Esther, show her the letter."

Esther took an envelope from her pocket. It had already been torn open. She didn't take out the letter. She rubbed the corner of the envelope with her thumb. "After Father died, Uncle Andrew wrote to send his condolences, and then he and I began a correspondence."

"Who's Uncle Andrew?" asked Lizzie.

"Father's cousin. Great-uncle Archibald's son. He came to Seattle once for business, but you were too little to remember."

Esther took something else from her pocket. A photograph. She slid it across the table. Lizzie looked at it and drew in a sharp breath: it was her father, dressed in a top hat and tuxedo with a white boutonniere. His wedding. She barely glanced at the other man—this Uncle Andrew—before pushing the photograph back. She didn't want a new uncle. Esther turned the photograph face down. "Uncle Andrew is an investor in a logging camp. It's in the Inside Passage, across from Vancouver Island, up in British Columbia. He's spending the summer there with Aunt Louise and their two sons. He wants to learn about the company and give his boys a chance to be in the woods. And he wants you to go with them."

Logging? *Canada?* "Are you joking?"

"You'd be doing lessons with the boys, who are seven and nine. I said you are very bright and would be perfect for the job."

"But I've never even been away from home by myself. Not even a night."

Esther pushed ahead. "You will earn one hundred dollars in two months, and that will be enough so you don't have to go to Portland. One hundred dollars would make up for not having boarders."

A hundred dollars.

Lizzie had inquired about a job as a floor girl at the millinery shop in the University District, but that only paid twenty cents an hour. Mary had a job as a babysitter for her neighbors, and that paid twenty cents for a whole afternoon.

"A hundred dollars?" she repeated.

"Uncle Andrew can afford to pay it," explained Thomas. "He's gotten rich investing Aunt Louise's money. He got lucky and sold stocks before the crash. She's from old San Francisco money. Honestly, I don't understand how she could be happy out there in the woods with a bunch of loggers."

Esther shot him a look. "I'm sure Aunt Louise is happy there. It must be beautiful."

Lizzie was too stunned to respond. Beauty had nothing to do with anything. Neither did a hundred dollars. She couldn't go to a logging camp in Canada by herself for a whole summer. She couldn't even make pork chops by herself, let alone survive in the woods.

"Why don't you think about it," said Thomas.

Robert cried out from his crib. Esther sighed and went to tend to him. Thomas said goodnight, and Lizzie was left alone in the kitchen with Uncle Andrew's letter.

I will meet her on June fifteenth at six in the evening at the Powell River Dock. She will be easy enough to identify I am certain. The date on the letter was the end of March. So Thomas and Esther had been sitting on this plan for two months. A secret, as if Lizzie were a child too young to understand. She folded the letter and pushed it back in the envelope. The return address was *Dark Water Bay Lumber Company, Dark Water Bay, Malaspina Inlet, B.C., Canada.* No roads, no numbers. Just water.

In the parlor, on the davenport, she smoothed sheets that had once been white but were now yellowed from wear. Her old bedroom had had pink sheets and matching pink-striped wallpaper. There had been a four-poster bed and pink, tulip-printed drawer liner in her dresser. Now she stored her clothes in a musty cabinet on one side of the davenport, her bedding and pillow in the other cabinet. She was diligent about keeping her belongings out of sight. "This is a parlor," Esther liked to remind her. "Not a bedroom."

Lizzie never slept well here. Street lamps glowed through the lace curtains. Smells from the kitchen lingered. Another family lived in the apartment upstairs, and the father worked late as a security guard. Every morning at four, his footsteps woke her.

She unbraided her hair, wound the ribbons around her thumb and index finger, and laid the coil at the base of the lamp. She combed through her long hair with her fingers, tugging out the snarls. Her brush was in the bathroom, and she didn't want to wake anyone.

Then, as she did every night, she pulled a *Popular Mechanics* magazine out from her pillowcase. Tucked inside was the last photograph of her family all together. Her mother was seated, and she held Lizzie, an infant in a bonnet, in her lap. Esther, ten years old, wore a white dress and a white floppy bow. She leaned against their mother so close as to nearly be in her lap as well. Their father was so tall, and their mother seated so low, that her head barely reached above his waist. He towered above his wife and daughters proudly, as if he were the first man in history to have a family.

On the back of the photograph, his handwriting was in ink that had faded to purple: *My loves. 1919*.

She pushed the photo back into the magazine and closed it. She rested her hand on the cover, an illustration of an airplane and sea cruiser. It was the last issue she'd gotten. Or rather, that her father had. Her name was on the address, but it was he who read each issue cover to cover. He talked her into weekend projects, such as building circuits and liquefying glue. Once, they'd made a radio because of a story about a park ranger using one to save himself from a bear.

Her father would want her to go to the logging camp. He'd tell her something to look forward to. A wood-cutting machine, or species of fish.

"I'll go," she said to him. "But only because I'm not wanted any place else."

CHAPTER
TWO

A week later, at five-thirty in the morning, Esther and Lizzie stood on the platform at the King Street Station. Lizzie clutched her suitcase, and Esther held Robert on her hip. His blue eyes were wide as he watched the commotion. Travelers bustled past in all directions. Metal screeched, and steam bellowed from Lizzie's train, which was nearly ready to depart.

"So you'll meet Uncle Andrew tonight at six," Esther shouted over the noise. "And then you will telephone me right away. I will be at the booth on the corner, so don't keep me waiting. Do you have your ticket?"

Lizzie nodded. They had bought it only ten minutes before, but she showed it again to her sister. Blue type on stiff white paper. $2.00 GREAT NORTHERN RAILWAY. ONE WAY ONLY.

"Do you have the six dollars?" Esther asked. She'd gone to the bank especially for Canadian dollars. Fifty cents for the trolley from the Vancouver train station to the ferry, one dollar and forty cents for the ferry to Powell River, and three dollars and ten cents left over for incidentals and emergencies. Lizzie had never had as much money in all her life, even when her father was still alive. She'd put the money in a pink silk coin purse embroidered with three roses. She was carrying the coin purse in the center of her suitcase. Esther didn't want her to carry a handbag because it would be too easy to steal or accidentally leave on a seat. Lizzie wore a pink floral print dress with a white sash and white sailor collar. Esther had added three extra inches to the sleeves and the skirt because Lizzie had grown since last summer. Esther had used second-hand napkins for the fabric so it would match how faded and thin the dress was.

Over the dress Lizzie wore a pink cardigan that she'd knit herself. Two white pom-poms the size of golf balls dangled cheerfully at the neck. On her feet were olive-green lace-up Oxfords with a flat heel. She'd wanted to wear her black Mary Janes to make a good impression, but Esther hadn't even let her pack them. "Think about what you'll want on your feet when you need to use an outhouse in the dark."

The train's whistle shrieked again. Esther jiggled Robert nervously. "I wish I had received another letter from Uncle Andrew, just to make sure the plan was still the same."

A man in a blue uniform with gold buttons yelled, "All aboard! Seattle to Vancouver!"

Lizzie rubbed Robert's cheek with the crook of her forefinger. "Goodbye, little peach." Then, waving to Esther's belly, she added, "Goodbye, whoever you are."

"All aboard!" the man repeated.

Esther and Lizzie embraced. Esther smelled of baby spit-up, cooking, and Ivory soap. Lizzie felt a tightening in her throat.

"Esther, I'm not sure—"

"Go on." Esther's voice was stern, but her eyes were filled with tears. "Train's leaving."

Lizzie marched up the narrow metal stairs and into the train car, where another uniformed man helped her lift her suitcase onto an overhead rack. She was able to find a window seat in time to wave goodbye to her sister and nephew as the train lurched away from the station.

And then they were gone.

As the train picked up speed, its wheels clattered in a two-beat rhythm. *A-lone, a-lone.* She felt herself begin to cry but then stopped because of the other passengers. She imagined what they would think. A twelve-year-old girl, too young to travel by herself. A bad family for sending her away, or something bad about her.

Across the aisle were a father and a little boy. The father read a newspaper. The boy fiddled with a toy car. He looked sad and bored. If she'd been on a train at that age with her father, he'd have read aloud to her, even from the newspaper.

When Lizzie had been in third grade, her father had stopped going to work. She didn't remember how long. Weeks. She'd stayed home too. They'd spent the days in the study with the shades drawn and only one lamp on. He'd read aloud old *Popular Mechanics.* If she had to choose one thing for Christmas, what would it be?

A heated birdhouse, or rocks to make the bathtub a turtle pond? At night, Lizzie heard her father cry in his bedroom. She guessed that he was missing Lizzie's mother, but she never asked.

Eventually, Mr. Underhill made her father go back to the office. When Esther found out about Lizzie's missing school, she was furious. Those first days back at school, when her father said goodbye, Lizzie screamed and called out after him. She was too old to do that, but she felt she'd die, or he would.

Lizzie looked out the window. They were in farmland now. Fog sat low over the fields. Everything was gray except for the telephone wires. Every so often there were houses. Not nestled in trees, but out in the open. She wondered about the families. They must be peculiar, to manage all alone.

Lizzie shouldn't have let her suitcase be put in the overhead rack. She wanted her book, which was packed inside. Mary had given it to her before she'd left. *Little Women*. Mary was going to read it too, so they'd think about each other all summer. Lizzie had read the first chapter the night before. It was about four daughters and their mother. They had to earn money because the father was away at war. The mother, Marmee, told the girls they had to carry their burdens like good pilgrims. Although Lizzie didn't understand what this meant, exactly, she liked the sound of it.

She wanted to read, but she didn't dare get the suitcase. It was heavy, and her arms were weak. She'd lose her balance, the way the train was rattling. And she didn't want to see what she'd tucked inside the book: the photograph of herself as a baby with Esther and her parents. She'd brought it because she didn't want to leave it behind, but that didn't mean she wanted to see it.

"The trolley's out of service. You have to take a taxi." Lizzie stood at an information kiosk at the Vancouver station. A man with bushy eyebrows and a gold-trimmed hat was explaining that there was no other way to the ferry dock.

"You're taking the two o'clock ferry?" he asked.

She nodded.

He looked at the clock behind them. It was a quarter past one. "Better run then. That's the last ferry of the day."

Her heart was pounding. Her face felt prickly and cold. But there was no time to panic. She made it to the street, where an automobile was driving past that had a sign on top that said TAXI. She flailed her arms and shouted, and it stopped for her. She clambered inside. Her seat smelled of sour milk and cigarettes.

"It'll be a dollar-fifty," said the driver, a bald old man with hairs on his neck.

"A dollar-fifty? The trolley was supposed to be fifty cents, but it's out of service, and—"

"That's the price. Take it or leave it."

He kept his grubby palm extended. She had to pay.

She made it to the ferry just as it was blasting its final boarding horn. It was about half the size of a Seattle ferry, and it looked less like a ferry and more like a long, narrow tugboat, with one steam stack and a single deck.

On board she paid her fare to a tall, skinny man in a uniform much shabbier than the men's on the train. In fact, it was barely a uniform at all but a brown shirt with B.C. FERRIES embroidered on the breast pocket.

"That'll be one-fifty," said the man in a bored monotone.

"I thought it was one-forty." That was what Uncle Andrew had written to Esther, and what Lizzie had seen posted at the dock as she had sprinted past.

"It's one-forty if you pay before you board."

She handed him the money, then counted what was left in her coin purse. Three dollars. Half of what she'd started with. There wasn't money left for any more bad luck. She snapped the coin purse shut and buried it back in her suitcase. She didn't want to think about money.

She made her way to a seat by a window that looked out to the ferry's deck. The deck was full of men. Men with shadowy eyes, men with oiled hair, men with shirts too far unbuttoned, revealing hairy chests. Men who carried soiled blankets rolled and tied with rope.

On the floor under the seat in front of her, jammed against the wall, she saw a newspaper. She lowered her head to look. The paper was filthy and covered in boot prints, but she could make out LOGGING TIMES. And a headline: "Investor Trouble at Dark Water Bay."

Dark Water Bay. Investor. Uncle Andrew.

She knelt down to get the paper, but as she reached under the seat, she realized the paper was soaking wet. The words of the article disappeared under a black puddle of water and cigarette butts. She couldn't read anything, or even touch the paper, without its falling apart.

The boat lurched, and she nearly fell face first into the newspaper puddle. She caught herself but didn't stand up. The boat rocked from side to side and bumped over another big wave. Smells of fish and gasoline had filled the boat. She snatched her suitcase and made it to the deck just in time. Her vomit caught on the wind, and she wiped her face with the sleeve of her sweater.

She closed her eyes and breathed in the cool, salty mist. Maybe the headline wasn't about her uncle. Maybe Dark Water Bay was big, like Elliot Bay, and there were many logging camps with many investors. Maybe her uncle was there to help with the trouble. Maybe the newspaper was trash from six months ago and the trouble was already resolved. Anyway, none of it mattered. She was going to tutor two little boys. Investments didn't concern her.

Maybe it would help to stretch her legs. She walked to a railing closer to the front of the boat. The boat was charging through a channel of steel-gray waves. Froth roared up on either side of the bow. A gull swooped overhead. Wind whipped Lizzie's braids against her cheeks, so she tucked them into the neck of her sweater.

When she'd taken the ferry to Bainbridge Island, where Mary's family spent their summers, there were homes on the shore. And children and picnics and bonfires. Even a lighthouse. But here, there was nothing and no one. Just rocks and trees. More trees than she could count in a lifetime.

When the boat arrived at Powell River Wharf, she was surprised it existed. How had people built it when there were no people? But there *were* people, at least a few. About a dozen men, similarly shabby to those arriving, were gathered there. Some waved. Most rocked on their heels and smoked.

The boat's engine idled, and the boat began to move slowly between barnacle-coated pilings. Pulsing around them in the green-black water were ghostly white figures with string-like fringes. Jellyfish. A bunch of kelp tangled around an underwater mooring line looked like a human head. The boat squealed against a piling. Men jumped off the ship and began securing it to the dock with thick ropes.

She didn't see anyone who looked like the man in the photograph. Then again, no one was wearing a suit and top hat, which was foolishly how she had been picturing him. Many men had beards; maybe he had grown one too. Maybe his hair had gone white. The picture was over twenty years old, after all.

The kelp on the mooring lines was rotting. The stench, mixed with gasoline and the slosh of the boat as it bounced in its own wake, made her want to sit down, but she forced herself to stay upright. The man who'd taken her fare helped her down a creaking ramp but didn't offer to carry her suitcase. Men around her were pushing wheelbarrows and balancing enormous loads in their arms: crates of beer, bags of potatoes, coils of metal cables. No one made eye contact. No one was her uncle.

Men started clearing out from the wharf. They were taking their loads uphill to trucks. She squinted. There, parked farthest away, was a black truck with letters barely legible under a layer of dirt. *Dark Water Bay.*

"Uncle Andrew?" she called when she reached the truck. She set her suitcase in a flat patch of dust. She stood up straight and smoothed her wind-tangled braids. "Andrew Parker?"

A bump came from within the truck, then a muffled grunt. Someone hopped onto the ground. A boy a few years older than she was. Dark brown eyes, black brows and lashes, high cheekbones, and a square jaw. Freckles covered his nose and cheeks. His skin was flushed and glistening with sweat. His shoulders were broad under his shirt, which must have once been striped but was now almost entirely sunbleached.

He regarded Lizzie casually, as if strange girls arrived all the time. "Andrew Parker left camp a month ago."

"But he was supposed to meet me here. I'm going to tutor his boys. I'm staying with him and Aunt Louise."

Now the boy looked at Lizzie with more interest. "Your aunt and the kids are gone too."

"But I'm supposed to meet them."

"Well, they're not here."

"Are you sure?"

"Positive."

It was impossible that she was alone. Impossible that she had traveled all this way to be here alone. She could hardly breathe. Her uncle had to be here. He *had* to.

The boy looked at her as if he were expecting her to turn around and go home. When she didn't, he turned toward the front of the truck and shouted, "Red! We've got someone who says she's Andrew Parker's niece."

There was a bang of metal and then a husky, annoyed answer. "Give me a minute! Can't leave the fan belt dangling."

The boy dug out a small circular tin from his pocket. The lid had a picture of a bright red flame. He swirled his finger in brown paste that reminded her of tea leaves. He smeared it under his lower lip. "Want some snoose?"

"No, thank you."

All I want is my uncle. And very soon, please.

A final clang and grunt. Then an old man appeared, black oil smeared across a faded blue jumpsuit. His fluff of hair was as white as cotton, his skin tanned and crumpled. His body was crooked and his gait uneven, but he moved with surprising speed. He was miniature, only a few inches taller than Lizzie and perhaps only a few pounds heavier.

His hands were dark with grease. He wiped his forehead with the inside of his wrist. His eyes were milky blue. Brown spots, like stains of tea, were splotched on his dry, wrinkled cheeks. His eyebrows were a few strands of white, his eyelashes mere stubs. He could have been a hundred years old.

"You're Andrew Parker's niece?" he asked. His voice was low and gravelly. His gaze was sharp and curious.

"Yes, sir," she nodded. *Let my uncle be here. Please say the boy is wrong.*

"Well, my girl, I'm sorry to say Andrew Parker and his family left for Vancouver a month ago."

"But I'm supposed to work for him. I received a letter."

Lizzie thought back to the letter, holding it at the kitchen table. The letter had been dated in March. And Esther hadn't heard anything from him since. Maybe her aunt and uncle really were gone.

No. No, no, no. It couldn't be true. It couldn't be true, but it was. She was here. Without an uncle, without enough money, without a way home. She could see the boy and the old man, and see them looking at her, but they didn't make her any less alone.

The man, Red, shook his head and whistled out a long breath as if someone had showed him an engine broken beyond repair. "Well, my girl, I don't know what to tell you. Where are you coming from?"

"Seattle."

Red looked over to the dock. She looked too. The ferry was still moored. The man who'd taken her fare was pacing the dock, smoking. There was still a chance to go back.

"How much money you got?" Red asked.

"Three dollars." That was enough for the ferry and the taxi but not the train. She needed five dollars for the whole trip. Maybe if the trolley was back in service she'd need less . . . No, there was no way she could get home without more money. Her only hope was if Red and the boy gave her some. She could pay them back. She could—

Red looked to the boy. "Got any dough left after the poker table?"

"Zero," he said, casting his eyes to the ground.

"I only got a quarter," said Red. "I just bought supplies and cleaned myself out."

Maybe someone else had money. She looked to the road, the beach, and the dock. But everyone was gone. The man in the brown uniform had gone back onboard. The ferry bellowed, and smoke shot up from the stack. The water churned behind the engine.

Esther. She needed to call Esther. "Is there a telephone?"

"Here? No siree." Red looked amused. He didn't understand how serious she was. How afraid she was to be alone.

"What if I go back to Vancouver? I can telephone my sister from there and have her send money."

"The money would take days. And the cheapest boarding house in Vancouver is two dollars a night."

"And that's not much of a place for a girl," added the boy. "Then again, neither is camp."

CHAPTER
THREE

Her thoughts were lifting into a dizzy fog. A logging camp. She was understanding, slowly, that that was where she was headed, no matter where her uncle had gone.

Red was talking. She had to listen. "The best you're going to be able to do is send a telegram from Mink Cove. The boss can do it."

"The boss?"

"Tertius Veil. He owns the camp. And that's where you're headed, unless you want to sleep on the beach. Help Freddie load the truck."

The boy, Freddie, stooped to pick up a white cloth sack with FLOUR stamped on it. Next to it was a crate marked POWELL RIVER PRODUCE. Sad leaves poked out through the slats, and a streak of green slime was smeared across the side. Another crate had a label for Old Goat Tobacco.

"Here."

Before she could move away, Freddie was shoving the flour sack into her arms. It was so large she could barely wrap her arms around it, and so heavy she nearly toppled over.

He took it back, lifting it as if it weighed nothing. "Just hit the john then," he said, annoyed.

"John?"

"Privy. It's on the beach," he said, tilting his head in that direction. "It's about a two-hour truck ride."

Two hours. It was unfathomable that there was a place even farther away than where she already was. But she made herself focus on what the boy was saying. A privy. She was too disoriented to feel embarrassed. To be honest, she was thankful. She had been too frightened to enter the foul-smelling closet on the ferry. High up the beach she found a narrow wooden outhouse under an overhang of trees. The whole structure leaned at a slant. No charming crescent moon was carved on the door.

She pulled up her skirt with one hand and pinched her nose with the other. She couldn't believe she was doing this. She couldn't believe she had woken up in Seattle, with a flush toilet and an embroidered hand towel, and little more than twelve hours later, she was here, urinating onto a pile of loggers' excrement.

By the time she returned to the truck, it was loaded.

"Red said the fan belt's fixed," reported Freddie, stepping onto the tailgate of the truck. The tailgate was rusted and caked with dust. A dented piece of metal dangled from the bumper.

He held out a hand, and she hesitated. She knew if she got in the truck, camp would be real. Also, she'd never held a boy's hand. Silly, to think of that now, but she did. The boy was handsome. Tanned, muscular. Not tall, and his nose was thick and jammed at a bit of an angle into his brow, but he was attractive. Capable.

"Come on," he said, thrusting his hand further toward her.

She grabbed it. His skin was warm, and he was as strong as he looked. She made it easily into the truck, ducking her head because the ceiling was low. Near the back, crates and sacks were stacked against the walls, emitting smells of tobacco, coffee, and vegetables. By the door was her suitcase, next to an ice chest streaked with what looked like blood. From a butcher, she hoped, and looked away.

Freddie slammed the back doors and latched them with a decisive *thwack*. Now there was little fresh air and barely any light, save from two small windows on the doors. She felt as if she were in prison.

"On your right," he instructed.

In the dim light, she could make out two boxes stacked to about knee height, with walls of boxes on either side. A small seat. She paused, but then, with a sudden growl, the truck lurched forward. She tumbled into her seat. The boxes by her head creaked. *Run*, she thought. She could find her things and escape, before it was too late. But she couldn't. She had no other place to go. The truck was on its way and taking her with it.

Freddie sat across from her, slid a low box between them, and rested his boots on it as if it were a footstool. He leaned his head against a crate and closed his eyes. No more conversation.

The truck picked up speed. It hit what sounded like a rock, and the floor bounced. Metal clanged and rattled. The air was smelling less like the water and more like the forest—and rubber and exhaust. Her stomach began to pitch. She took a handkerchief from her pocket and placed it over her nose. The smell of Ivory flakes reminded her of home, of Esther scrubbing laundry in the yard, of Robert's tiny shirts hung to dry.

Esther. She was waiting for Lizzie's telephone call. Was she worried? Why hadn't their uncle written to say he'd left camp? What had Red said about a telegram and sending money? There were too many questions, and Lizzie was too tired to think.

She looked at Freddie's boots. They came up nearly to his knees, with laces circled many times at the top. She could see the tops of the boots because his pants were cropped and cuffed. As her eyes adjusted to the darkness, she noticed that a hole had been worn through the toe of one boot. The sock beneath it was thick with filth. On the boot's sole she saw rows of short spikes, as if nails had been punched through from inside.

She noticed her own clothes. Her pink pom-pom sweater and pink sailor dress. Her canvas Oxfords and white stockings. To think that she'd wanted to wear her Mary Janes.

At her father's memorial service she'd worn her Mary Janes. During the whole service she had pushed her shoes together and looked at the space in between them. She had felt her shoulders tight against her body and had imagined her body slipping through the space between the shoes, slipping deep below the floor. Not to a destination, just . . . away.

She listened to the truck jiggle and rattle. She listened to Freddie snore. She listened to the crates creak. She didn't let her attention settle anywhere for too long.

Finally, the truck stopped.

Freddie jolted awake and opened the doors without communicating anything except a grunt. She forced herself to stand up. Like after the memorial service. Stand up. Pretend. Outside the sky was dark, and she heard her surroundings before she saw them. The splashing of waves against rocks, the hollow lap of water under a dock, the creak of a boat. Her stomach growled. She hadn't eaten anything since breakfast, and she had vomited that over the side of the ferry.

Red emerged from the cab of the truck. He wore a thick knit hat, and without his fluff of hair he was even shorter. His white brows were the most visible part of his face in the darkness. He raised them as his gaze traveled toward the water. Then, footsteps and the squeak of wheels came from the dock. With the help of the half moon, she made out a tall figure pushing a wheelbarrow toward them.

"That's Olavfur," said Red. "He's going to take us to camp."

They still weren't there. She felt tears coming, but she pressed them down.

The stranger—this Olavfur—spoke to Red first, then the two of them came around to the back of the truck.

Olavfur appeared older than Esther and Thomas but not yet middle-aged. A knit hat like Red's was pulled down around his ears. His features were square and well-proportioned. Good-looking, if his jaw hadn't been set in such an icy manner.

"This is Lizzie," said Red. "Andrew Parker's niece."

Olavfur looked at Red. "She shouldn't go to camp." He had an accent. *Shoo-dn't goo.* His tone was angry—not at her, but at Red.

"No choice," said Red.

Olavfur regarded her for a long time. He seemed to want to say something but was holding back. Finally he looked away. He told Red and Freddie, "Unload." *Un-loot.*

Olavfur was as strong as Red and Freddie combined, and the boat was loaded quickly. It was about as large, or small rather, as the truck. It had an outboard motor. There was no roof on the main part of the boat. Only the driver and passenger seats were covered.

"The bottom of the boat's the safest, Miss," instructed Red, giving her a hand as she stepped cautiously over the gap between the dock and the boat. The hull tilted under her feet, but she managed not to fall.

"Sit on anything," said Red. She found the least revolting thing, the sack stamped FLOUR, and sat carefully. The boat smelled of mildew and fish. Fishhooks and cigarette butts were scattered at her feet. White flecks. Bird droppings? She saw her suitcase, which wasn't smeared with blood or other grime, thank goodness, and she felt momentarily comforted. But then, seeing it there made this whole journey seem real. This suitcase had started this morning in Seattle and was now . . . here.

Olavfur stood behind the wheel. Although there were driver and passenger seats, neither he nor Red sat. Olavfur flicked a switch, and Lizzie saw two colored lights reflected in the water at the bow of the boat. Red on the left, green on the right. Freddie untied the boat from the tiny dock, pushed off with his foot, and hopped inside. He sat opposite from her, cramped between the face-down wheelbarrow and the Old Goat Tobacco crate.

The boat's motor was louder than the truck's. The sound echoed across the water. The wake was surprisingly big. She peered over the side and saw the V-shaped lines of foam, visible in their whiteness, until the booming rise and fall of the boat, and the whipping wind in her hair, made her crouch back down.

Olavfur steered with little movement. The pointed bow raised up and sliced smoothly through the flat water. Above her were more stars than she had ever seen. She couldn't decide whether the space between the stars was as pure a black as she had ever seen or barely black at all, given the light of the stars blurring together.

After about half an hour, the motor slowed abruptly. The bow came down and the boat puttered into a harbor. Floating on the bay's surface was a huge raft, a ballroom floor, of tree trunks bound together, each tree longer than the dock, many times as long as the boat. As the wake rippled underneath the logs, they thunked against each other.

Olavfur guided the boat next to the dock, avoiding two rowboats, an outboard motor boat, and a sailboat. Freddie hopped onto the dock and secured their boat with a series of knots. Olavfur lifted the wheelbarrow onto the dock by himself with one motion. The men began unloading the supplies. They moved as if they had each inch of the dock memorized.

She gazed at the camp. There was enough moonlight to see a great deal. The tide was high, the water tight up to the reeds at the top of the beach. Beyond the beach, at the edge of the forest, stood a row of what looked like one-room log cabins. White paint rimmed square windows and pitched roofs. A larger, more substantial building sat apart from the cabins and higher up from the beach. She thought of a town a child might build from a set of blocks. Surrounding everything was forest. A single, living mass. All sound, light, and breeze seemed sucked back by it. In school she had learned about the story of man versus nature. If she were in that kind of story, the forest would win.

From one of the cabins came a thrum of low-toned, shouting laughter. Not gaiety, but something darker. Jeering. Men.

The supplies were gone from the dock now, and only Red remained. He reached his hand to Lizzie, who was still sitting in the boat. "Up you go," he said.

"I can't." She felt the boat would tip over without the weight of the men and the supplies. The water was pure black, and she could barely see the difference between the dock and the water.

"You can." He gestured again, but she still didn't lift her hand. She felt embarrassed to be disobedient, but she couldn't make herself move.

Red spoke again. "It's hard to balance now that there's no cargo. So bend your knees as you stand, and don't put all your weight onto your toes."

The words *knees* and *toes* had an effect. They made her want to test those body parts, to see if she could stand up. She held on to the wall of the hull, pushed herself up, and kept her knees relaxed. Once she was steady, with her heels weighted and not too much pressure on the toes, she stood without falling, even though the hull sloshed from side to side. She almost— just almost—smiled.

"Atta girl," said Red. "Now hop out."

Fearing the small chasm between the boat and the dock, she accepted Red's hand.

Once she was standing on the dock, her legs rubbery from the boat, Red said, "Let's find you a bed."

A bed. Lizzie hadn't thought about this. In one of the cabins? With the men?

Red explained nothing, and Lizzie didn't have the nerve to ask. She followed him down the dock and onto the land. At the edge of the woods he had set her suitcase and a lantern. He struck a match on a rock and lit the lantern, which went *hiss* and then *poof*. He charged up a narrow path into the woods, the lantern swinging on a squeaky handle, her suitcase in his other hand. She scrambled to keep up. The yellow light illuminated rocks, moss, tree roots, and then a heap of nails. A pile of rusty chains. A saw leaning against a stump. An ax.

"Do you have any skills?" he asked.

"Skills?"

"Do you do anything useful?"

Lizzie wanted to laugh out loud. She couldn't even cook pork chops. "I don't think so," was all she could think to say.

Red sighed. She wished he would say, "It will work out," or "You'll be all right," but he said nothing, just marched ahead into darker and darker woods. She could barely hear the men's voices at all.

They reached a small structure. A roof of shaggy bark lay limply atop four walls of crooked, overlapping boards. There was no door except for a panel of canvas, which Red drew to the side.

"Boat shed." He gestured with his lamp as if to say, "Step inside."

This was where her bed was? Here? She hesitated before sidling past the canvas panel into a room the size of a pantry. She was met by odors of must, dampness, and decaying metal. Hooked to the walls and strewn on the ground was an emporium of boat-type things: ropes, sails, buckets, fishing rods, fishing nets. A hammer and ax were propped against—what was that? A tree stump?

Right inside of the room, like a table. An outboard motor, standing in the corner, looked like a horse head.

Red set down her suitcase and passed her the lantern. He untangled a web of ropes that was nailed to the wall, extended it to another nail across the little room, and she could see the ropes were a hammock. Red padded it with a sheet of stiff fabric.

"Extra blanket," he said, pointing to a tall spool of cloth that she thought might be a sail. He gestured to the hammock. "Go on. Test out your bed."

She looked at the pathetic walls, some boards not even meeting the ground. She drew in a breath and maneuvered herself into the hammock. The ropes creaked, but nothing fell down.

"Keep your clothes on," said Red. "Add whatever extra you have. Protect against the bugs. Vermin will stay on the floor. Goodnight then." With that, he flapped through the canvas door and left, taking his lantern and leaving her in total darkness.

She heaved herself forward, to get out. He couldn't leave, not like this. But the hammock was deep, and she was stuck. And it didn't matter. Red couldn't help her. Nothing could. Half-crying, half-asleep, she listened all night to the soft splash of the waves and infinite darkness of the trees.

CHAPTER
FOUR

Lizzie climbed into her father's car. She put her book bag at her feet.

"It's nice there," said her father, looking out the car's window to Esther and Thomas's house. It was a wet, silvery night. Lamps glowed through the lace curtains. Lizzie had stayed there for dinner, as she had nearly every night for weeks. Her father couldn't afford the housekeeper anymore, and he rarely cooked—or ate.

"You'd be happy there," he said. "They're a real family."

Lizzie should've said that she was happy already, with him. That they already were a real family. But she hadn't said anything.

The car hovered at the edge of Lizzie's sleep. She didn't like it there. She woke carefully, piecing things together first by smell. Chimney smoke. Maybe bacon. She opened her eyes. Cobwebs hung thick in the corners of the room. The blade of an old circular saw was nailed to the wall. It looked like a rusted sun.

She hadn't forgotten where she was, yet she was still surprised. The only thing that felt real was her body. It ached from the hammock. All night the ropes had pressed into her thighs and shoulders. Her lower back was cramped from being curved in the same place for hours.

A bell clanged, and she heard men's voices at a distance. Breakfast. There was definitely food in the smoke smell. She had no appetite, but she wondered whether the boss, who could send the telegram, would be there. And she would have to leave the shed sometime. It might as well be now.

She spat on her fingers to wipe off the night's tears and hastily pulled on a fresh dress. The fabric was printed with small yellow and blue flowers, and even in the murky light she could tell the fabric was creased. She unbraided her hair, brushed it, and re-braided it. She could feel dust left over from the truck ride.

Now or never. She swept aside the canvas curtain.

But as soon as she felt the cool morning against her skin, as soon as she saw the trees and smelled the dirt, her resolve faded. She looked at herself through the eyes of a logger. A silly girl in a silly city dress. An orphan without enough money to go home. A girl whose own uncle had abandoned her.

Just as she was about to go back into the shed, she heard a creak.

There, across a rocky knoll, was Red, stepping out of a wooden box that looked like a coffin. "Mornin'!" he said, stretching his arms over his head and yawning.

She could barely believe her eyes. "Did you *sleep* in there? Is that a coffin?"

"You betcha. I made it myself with top-grade cedar. Figured I should get used to it. I'm nearly eighty." He swept his arm grandly to indicate their surroundings. "'Death is the king of this world: 'Tis his park where he breeds life to feed him.' That's George Eliot."

Lizzie didn't know what to say. She had never in a million years imagined seeing a man sleeping, on purpose, in a coffin. Or quoting George Eliot, whoever that was.

"Come along, Miss Lizzie. Let us break the fast."

She hurried to keep up as she followed him down the hill toward a large structure. The chimney billowed with smoke that blended into the morning's pale sky. On either side of the path were trees that might have been Christmas trees, except they were much, much bigger. Some trunks were as wide as she was tall, and they grew so high that she would have had to stretch her neck to see their tops. Beneath the trees, on the side of the path, were light brown brambles and bushes dotted with red berries. Rocks jutted through the soil, reminders that the beach was close by. On the rocks grew orange and yellow moss.

Farther down the path, there were fewer trees and more stumps—and a row of five cabins. Or, half-tents, half-cabins. Their bottom halves were wooden clapboard, their top halves pitched tarpaulins. They had porches, and from their railings hung thick socks. A dozen or so pair per cabin. From one railing dangled a pair of boxing gloves.

"Do you like novels?" asked Red.

"Pardon me?"

"Novels. Do you read them?"

What was a logger doing asking her about novels? "Yes. I'm reading *Little Women* right now."

"Ahh! Jo March, what a heroine."

Lizzie couldn't help but smile, imagining Red liking Jo March, the tomboy of the March family. What would Jo make of a logging camp? She might be pleased by the adventure—but also scared. Lizzie was scared. That's what she was. She had no money. She was alone. A sick, hollow feeling came over her, but she kept walking.

Inside the cookhouse were the men. There must have been nearly fifty, crowded at four long tables and hunched over plates. Their clothes were gray and brown. Most wore striped shirts and suspenders, and some added canvas jackets or thick sweaters. Many wore hats. Frayed slouch hats, or floppy leather hats with wide brims. On the heads without hats, hair hung in oily chunks.

"Welcome!" shouted a dark-haired man, and he saluted her with his coffee mug. He and the men sitting near him laughed. Another logger spat tobacco on the floor and gave her a look halfway between flirtation and threat. A bald man grinned at her with rotten, stumpy teeth.

These men weren't Paul Bunyans. More like street rats.

She felt so on display that she was nearly compelled to wave, but instead she ducked her head and looked at

Red's heels as he walked ahead. She noticed the same metal spikes she had seen on Freddie's boots. The spikes made scratching noises on the filthy, wide-planked wood floor, which, she now saw, was gashed with marks in all directions, as if by wild cats.

All around were sounds of the cookhouse. A chaos of voices and laughter, plates and silverware, chairs dragging against the floor, heavy boots. She focused hard on Red's heels and imagined pushing the noises away from her, forming a tunnel around her, protecting her from the men.

Please, God. She wasn't religious, but that was how the words came to her. *Please, God. Just let me survive.*

Red led them to a table at the back of the room. There sat the boy from the day before, Freddie. He nodded casually, as if he'd seen her a hundred times before, and went back to his eating. Next to her sat a group of men speaking loudly in an accent. Scottish? It was so thick, she could barely tell the words were English.

"Mud?" asked Red after they'd seated themselves.

"He means coffee," Freddie said.

"No, thank you. But I would like some . . . " She looked around the table. In a casserole dish were beans and gravy. Both were the same shade of gray, and lumps of white jelly floated in the gravy. "Just water please."

She sipped from her cup while Red and Freddie ate without speaking. Long white hairs hung below Red's nostrils and curled from his earlobes. White stubble gathered in patches on his cheeks and the loose skin of his neck, like snow patches on a mountain. Freddie's coloring was as vivid as Red's was pale. His dark hair, with an auburn sheen in the light, was thick. The freckles that spread thickly across his nose and cheeks, instead of making him look childish, radiated sun and labor. A boy of the outdoors. A boy who couldn't care less about a girl in a flowered dress and braided pigtails.

She wanted to write to Mary to say she'd met the most handsome boy of her life at the same time she'd met a man who slept in a coffin.

"Will I be able to send my telegram today?"

"Not from here, Miss," said Red. "The boss has to go into Mink Cove. And he isn't here today. Off to Rachel Bay, I heard, to settle some business about tugboats."

"When will he return?"

"Suppertime, I imagine. But I found something to do with you in the meantime."

A tall, narrow woman appeared at the side of the table. She wore a crisp white apron over a faded brown gingham dress. Her rain-cloud-gray hair was rolled into an old-fashioned bun. Her skin was powdered with rouge. Her receding chin brought to mind Eleanor Roosevelt.

"Pipe down!" she hollered to the maybe-Scotsmen, and they obeyed. She eyed Lizzie suspiciously. "So this is our penniless girl?"

"I think she has some nickels." Red winked at Lizzie. "Lizzie, this is our cook, Gladys."

"Nice to meet you," said Lizzie.

"You've done laundry before, I imagine?" Gladys asked.

Once. Lizzie had put Esther's favorite blouse through the wringer and cracked its mother-of-pearl buttons. "Yes," Lizzie answered.

"Good. Wait for me on the porch."

As the men shuffled out of the cookhouse to start their day in the woods, Lizzie sat alone on the porch behind the kitchen. In a nearby clearing stood a contraption of timber and tree branches, from which hung a massive cauldron, and below it was a stone-circled fire pit. Was a witch working there? Water sputtered over the cauldron's brim and sizzled into the flames. The steam smelled like vinegar, but worse.

Whack! She couldn't tell whether the noise was from the fire or something else. Then she heard it again, and the porch rattled. She looked behind her. At the far end of the porch, Olavfur was banging something against the handrail.

He nodded for her to come over. She remembered what he'd said the night before about how she shouldn't be at camp. She wanted to say that she was busy with the laundry, but she was obviously not.

"Girl," he said. *Gerl.* He nodded again.

On shaky legs she walked to him, but she stopped before she got too close. Another whack. It was a glove, turned inside out. He whacked again, and from the glove came a cloud of sawdust and wood chips. She felt the dust in her nose and eyes.

He picked the last stray wood chips from the leather, then turned the glove right side out. He tucked the glove, with its mate, under his suspender by his shoulder. His hands were calloused and cut. He looked at her. His cornflower-blue eyes were vivid against his tanned skin. Blond eyebrows went straight across above them, at perfect right angles with his nose. His lips were wide and full.

"The men are not good," he said. *Nut goot.* "You are a little girl."

He held her gaze somberly before picking up his ax, which had been leaning against the railing. The steel edges glinted in the sun. He balanced the long handle over one shoulder as if he were a baseball player with a bat. Without any more explanation, he walked in the direction of the other men. As she watched the Y of suspenders on his large back, she felt a chill on her skin, despite the smoke from the fire. She wanted him to stay, to protect her—but perhaps he himself was one of the bad men.

The kitchen's screen door slammed, and Gladys emerged onto the porch. She was carrying a sack of laundry that seemed to weigh as much as she did.

"Oomph," she said as she dropped it next to Lizzie. Even through the bag, she could smell sweat, maybe even urine.

Gladys went to the cauldron and, with a long, fat stick, scooped out the clothes that had already been boiled. Pants, undershirts, long underwear. They were steaming. She dropped them into a metal tub and pushed the tub toward the porch with the instep of her shoe. Her spindly, stockinged legs were stronger than they appeared.

She handed Lizzie a hard-bristled brush, lifted a shirt from the tub, and pulled back its collar to show a ring of brown. "Scrub necks and cuffs especially." Then she located a place near the elbow where the fabric was bunched on itself, as if caught around a wad of chewing gum. "Pitch needs to be removed because it tears the fabric. Check the seats of the trousers especially. Those savages sit on any old log. And use that." She pointed to a bottle of clear liquid next to Lizzie.

Gladys shook the bag of dry laundry into the cauldron, pressed the clothes down with her stick, and went back into the kitchen.

Alone, Lizzie looked at the brush and the steaming tub. She should've told Gladys she didn't know how to do laundry. She certainly didn't know how to do *this* laundry.

She held up the bottle of clear liquid. The label said KEROSENE. That was for fires, she thought, not laundry. She looked around. There was another bottle of a white cream that was labeled LYE SOAP. That must've been what Gladys meant.

Lizzie poured the soap on the brush. Immediately she coughed. She felt burning in her throat and eyes. She turned her face to catch her breath and waited a moment before starting to scrub. Even then, she kept her face turned as she scrubbed the pitch. Her hands stung and grew red. But she was making little progress with the pitch. In fact, all her tugging back and forth was wadding up the pitch even more. She did another scrub, and the fabric around the pitch tore open.

"Lizzie! What are you doing?" Gladys stood on the porch and coughed. "Are you using the lye?" She stooped down and picked up the bottle of kerosene. "This is what I told you to use."

"I thought it was for the fire. I used the stuff called soap."

"That's nearly pure lye. I just put a bit in with the water. I'm surprised you haven't burned right through your hands. Let me see them." Lizzie showed her hands, which were bright red and starting to blister.

"Let me see what you did there." Lizzie showed where she'd torn the shirt. "That's why we use the kerosene," said Gladys. "It dissolves the pitch so you don't have to scrub so hard."

Gladys didn't sound angry so much as disappointed. Lizzie was going to be no help after all. "I can finish up," Gladys said. "Do you want cold water, for your hands?"

"No thank you." All she wanted was to be alone.

She hurried through the woods to her shed. But there, she couldn't bring herself to push aside the canvas curtain. The morning sun was bright. Even from outside, she could smell fish and baking rust.

She slumped onto a rock and let the tears come. There had been so many tears last night, but there were still more. More and more and more. She held her face in her hands, which burned worse than a sunburn and smelled worse than vinegar, and the crying didn't stop. Laundry was a simple job. Esther would've known what to do, but Lizzie knew nothing.

Except that she didn't want to go back into that shed.

Once she'd run out of tears, she peered around the side of the shed and spotted something that looked like a small path. She decided to follow it. Soon the forest thinned, and low tree boughs and waist-high bushes crowded the passage. The path became littered with pebbles, and then, abruptly, it descended with a cool rush of breeze. She emerged onto a high section of the beach, a plateau of rock that offered a view of the entire Dark Water Bay.

To her right was the dock where she had arrived the night before. There were the hundreds of logs, stretching over a quarter or a third of the bay. They were like Lincoln Logs dumped into a bathtub and bound together into a single surface. The largest logs were as wide as Model Ts and seemed as long as city blocks. Their ends were sawed clean, no trace of widening or narrowing; these logs were sections of trees taller than she could comprehend.

. She saw where the logs had come from. Up the beach from the logs was a steep channel of bare hillside with a railroad-looking track running down it. High above the track, cables were strung between trees as if they were cables for trolleys.

And there were men working. She could hear them better than she could see them. They shouted. Clanged metal. Splashed things into the water. Men on the dock worked with ropes from the raft of logs. The bay was an outdoor factory.

Suddenly she realized that if she could see the men, they could see her. She ducked behind a tall rock. She sat down on the flattest rock she could find and was surprised how hot it was through her thin dress.

The whole beach was hot. As bright and dry as it had been dark and wet the night before. The tide was way, way out, so far out that the ramp to the dock was at an incline steeper than a staircase. A poor purple starfish, normally deep underwater, was drying out in the sun. Brown kelp, long tails with bulb heads, clustered at the shoreline with a film of yellow foam. Everywhere the smells of fish and hot salt.

She was pleased to be alone. Not alone in the shed, or alone with laundry, but alone with no one watching or expecting something of her. She hadn't realized how tired she had become. Her body was sore from the hammock and the laundry, and her brain was sore from the fear and worry. Her body was giving up. The harbor, in its strange heat, was taking her over.

Below her was a tide pool. The water was clear and deep. She slid closer to the pool and plunged her hands in. Never had cool water felt so good. She spread out her red fingers and rested them on the pebbles. A green crab the size of a bottle top scuttled over her thumb. She splashed water on her face and immediately spat. Salt! She dabbed some on the back of her neck.

She looked down the length of the beach in both directions. No one. She wriggled her toes in her Oxfords. Their canvas was olive green, the piping and laces beige, but she could barely tell the colors apart because they were both caked in dirt. A blister was developing on her left big toe, another starting on the heel.

Then, quick as a wink, she unsnapped her garter belt through her skirt and wriggled out of her stockings.

Both feet of her stockings were so filthy that it looked as if she had stained them with tea. She dunked them under the water and wrung them out, watching the dirt puff out into the clear green water. Then she slipped her bare feet into the water. It was surprisingly cool. She rubbed dirt out from between her toes. How she longed for a true bath.

She thought of her bathroom in Seattle, its white porcelain sink and white towels with yellow embroidered roses. The floor was black-and-white hexagon tiles. She could practically smell Thomas's sandalwood shaving soap and Esther's Lily of the Valley perfume oil. She could practically feel the smooth, shiny spout of the faucet. Taste the fresh water.

Home. That was the word that came into her mind, but it wasn't the right word. Without her uncle, she wouldn't earn the hundred dollars. She would be sent off to Portland. Another place that wasn't home.

Lizzie heard splashing. She looked up and saw a boat.

CHAPTER
FIVE

The boat came from around a rock that jutted into the bay. The boat was backlit by the sun, and Lizzie had to squint, but there was Red, with his small stature and fluff of white hair. The vessel was larger than a dinghy, but he was rowing. As he came closer, she could see that the boat had a motor, tipped out of the water, its propeller tilted up into the air.

"Reel me in?" he yelled.

"Me?" She looked around the beach. The loggers were too far down the beach to hear.

"Yeah, you!" Red stood up in the boat, and the hull sloshed side to side. Then he took one oar, as if he were a gondolier, and began pushing it against the rocks underneath him, inching closer to the shore.

With the other hand, he held a coil of thick rope. "Ready?"

She stepped over seaweed and slick rocks to the water's edge. One end of the rope whipped through the air and thunked at her feet like a dead snake. She picked it up. It was cold and slimy.

"Pull!" said Red. She was sure the boat was much too heavy, but she yanked on the rope anyway. To her surprise, the boat floated forward easily. One more big tug and the bow scraped gently onto the shore and came to a stop.

"Give me a hand," he said. The rocks tipped under her feet, so she bent her knees and balanced her weight like he'd taught her to do on the boat the night before. She extended her hand, and Red grabbed it. His grip was strong, but his fingers felt like mere bones. For the split second that she helped support his weight, she could tell how small he was. Closer to her size than Freddie's. But Red was fast and had steady balance. He jumped to the beach without soaking his boots.

"Well done!" he grinned.

She smiled too. She had to admit, she felt a little proud.

With a series of tugs and tightenings, he tied the rope around a tall rock farther up the beach. She could see that the boat was in bad shape: splintered wood, rusted metal prow, a slimy bucket she assumed was for bailing if the boat filled with water. Frankly, she was surprised Red had made it anywhere at all.

After Red snugged the last knot, he wiped the water from his palms onto the thighs of his coveralls. "That'll do her. And tomorrow I can cover her with a tarpaulin. But I wanted to get her out of the water so she didn't keep rotting away. Thank you for your help."

"Certainly."

"Sit with me while I smoke? The outboard leaks gas when I lift it, which poses a problem not only for the motor but also for my habit."

Red sat on a large, flat rock. There was another next to it, so Lizzie sat there. He reached for his chest pocket, pulled aside one of his suspenders, and took out a cigarette. It was like all the cigarettes at camp, crumpled and hand-rolled. His fingertips were yellow.

Red pulled a match from his pocket and struck it on the rock. The flame burned into the paper as Red pushed the match against the cigarette and sucked the other end. He put nearly half the cigarette into his mouth and drew in a deep breath. His eyes closed, as if he were listening to music.

He opened them again and looked at his boat. "There are shipworms eating that poor thing. I need to take it out of the water to dry the wood. But they aren't worms, you know. They're long clams. They're eating the dock too, but the boss is too cheap to do anything about it."

Cheap. She thought of the newspaper headline: "Investor Trouble." She wanted to ask Red what had happened to her uncle. But at the ferry dock, he hadn't seemed to know anything. And she was ashamed. *She* should be the one to know what had happened to her own uncle, not some logger. She dug the toe of her shoe into some pebbles.

Red took a long drag, then blew it out slowly, wiggling his shoulders. Then he rummaged through a heap of empty oyster shells. The shells were strewn nearly everywhere on the beach. He turned over a half shell and tapped his cigarette ash into it.

"So, how was the laundry?" he asked.

"Terrible. That's why I'm here."

"Ahh." Red smiled but didn't laugh. "Well, you'd never done loggers' laundry before."

"I haven't really done *any* laundry before. My father's housekeeper always did it, and then my sister. The one time I did it, I ruined a sweater."

Now Red did laugh, but gently. "Oh, who doesn't ruin a sweater now and then. But what about your mother? Didn't she do laundry?"

"I don't know. She died of the flu when I was a baby."

He raised his sparse white eyebrows, then took another suck on his cigarette.

"Do you have parents?" she asked. Immediately she regretted the question. Of course he did. But they'd be dead. *He* was nearly dead.

"What d'you think, girl? They're arriving by boat tomorrow."

"Really?" She imagined two ghostly people rowing ashore, waving.

"I'm teasing," Red laughed. "They're dead and gone. My father was a farmer, and my mother raised six children to adulthood. Up in Maine. But I was the youngest son, and too little to be of much help. So as soon as I could, I set out west, working on the railroads."

"How old were you?"

"Oh, your age. Somewhere around there. Old enough to learn how to lay track."

She couldn't imagine someone her own age leaving home and not even going to a relative. "Did you like it?"

"Well enough. I liked being outdoors, that was certain. I was too small to carry much track, so that's how I learned to work on engines, which I liked. Still do. That was a piece of luck."

"When did you read *Little Women*?" she asked.

"A long time ago. I'm indiscriminate with what I read. Women, men, adventure, romance—I steal 'em all."

"Steal?"

"Well, I haven't had much luck recently. But when I worked on the rails, it was paradise. The first morning I hopped aboard, I found a copy of George Eliot's *Middlemarch* in the train station, abandoned on a bench. So I took it, and it kept me company my whole way to Montana. I think I found *Little Women* somewhere in Idaho. My mother was a schoolteacher, you see, and I was her baby. So I had no choice but to sit and be taught to read."

Lizzie liked imagining Red nestled beside his mother in a snowy cabin in Maine. She wondered if he'd ever seen her again, after the railroads. But she didn't want to ask, in case he hadn't.

Suddenly Red coughed the loudest cough she'd ever heard, as if stones were popping in his chest. He turned away to hack up spit on some rocks. He wiped his mouth on the shoulder of his shirt. "Did you know George Eliot was really a woman, and she changed her name?"

Lizzie had never heard of her. "In real life, or just for writing?"

"Just for writing, I think. But I like George for a woman in real life."

"Me too. Like Jo. She just cut her hair."

"Good ole Jo. She's tough—like you."

"I'm tough?" All she had done was cry.

"You've made it this far, haven't you?"

Red returned to the woods, but Lizzie couldn't bear to spend the rest of the afternoon in the shed. Instead, she laid out one of the torn sails on a patch of grass, lay on it, and read. She spotted an apple tree and ate three apples for lunch. She even managed a nap, although she woke to find ants crawling up her legs. She considered working on her new niece's or nephew's soakers, which she'd packed, but she didn't want to think about a baby she wouldn't grow up with once she was sent to Portland.

By evening, the day's despair left her with little appetite. Although she smelled cooking on the wood smoke and heard men clamber into the cookhouse, she didn't join them. Too many mosquitoes were finding her bare legs, so she went inside the shed. There, enough light slanted through the holes that she was able to read some more.

Then, outside, footsteps rustled though the reeds. There was heavy breathing, then a knock on wood next to the canvas curtain. The whole shed rattled.

"Miss Parker? It's Tertius Veil. The camp's boss."

Boss Veil. Here. Lizzie's hand shook as she patted her hair and smoothed her dress. Her stockings! She'd balled them up under a sweater. It was not yet dark, but the sun had faded some. Maybe he wouldn't notice her bare legs.

"Anybody home?" the man's voice asked. Lizzie wanted to hide, but there was no choice. She pulled back the canvas curtain.

An older, rotund man in a bowler hat dipped his head in greeting. He had a puffy white mustache and wide, lumpy cheeks. Sunk deep into their sockets, his eyes were small slits. His nose protruded sharply from his brow like an animal's snout. His black suit was faded and worn, and it was too snug around the waist. Nonetheless, the ensemble could have served as formal dress compared to the loggers' clothes.

"So this is Andrew Parker's niece." His expression was flat, almost as if he'd been expecting her.

"Yes, I'm Lizzie Parker. Nice to meet you boss—Mister—"

"You can call me Boss Veil like the men do. Come on. Get your things. This shed is no place for a little girl."

He said it in a way that made her feel humiliated, as if she'd chosen to sleep in the shed. Hurriedly, she stuffed her clothes into her suitcase. She was careful to pack her coin purse despite its meager contents.

Boss Veil went ahead, carrying her suitcase. Although he was a decade or two younger than Red, he walked more slowly and with worse balance. He wore fancy leather shoes instead of the men's spiked boots.

She called ahead to him, "I'm sorry I'm here. I don't have money to go home, but I can get some. My sister can wire it, if I send her a telegram."

The word *money* felt horrible coming from her mouth. Crass. That's what Esther said about a woman discussing money. Lizzie couldn't bring herself to say exactly how much she needed: two dollars, to go with the three she already had. Maybe more if there were going to be any more surprises.

"We'll sort that out tomorrow," he said. His voice was oddly blank, as if he didn't care about the money. Or that she was at camp at all. Or perhaps he was just tired.

She followed him past the cookhouse and up a slight hill to a house the size of all the loggers' cabins combined. The shingles were light-colored and crisp, not dingy from weather and moss. Royal blue paint brightened the window trims and door. She and Boss Veil climbed onto the porch. It was as sturdy and quiet as the cookhouse's was saggy and squeaky.

"Sss!" hissed Boss Veil. He looked toward his shoes and kicked something. A black cat skittered off the porch and meowed in the bushes.

A man's voice came from inside. "Boss?"

"Brought the girl," announced Boss Veil, opening the door. He motioned for Lizzie to enter first.

She didn't see the source of the voice, just a large room that seemed to function as parlor, dining room, and kitchen all in one. A davenport and armchair cozied themselves around a rag rug and stone fireplace, in which a small blaze was crackling. Against another wall was a small kitchen: pot-bellied stove, pots and colanders dangling from the ceiling, and wooden shelves neatly stacked with dishes and cans. Across from the kitchen, behind a long dining table, was a view of the sunset. Orange light glinted off emerald water. Far-off islands looked black yet outlined by fire.

Suddenly Lizzie felt a presence at her side. She turned to find the tallest man she had ever seen. She had to step back to see his face. He was younger than Boss Veil but older than Esther. His ebony hair was combed slickly back. His eyes were algae green, and his lashes were thick and black. His face revealed no emotion. He looked at her but said nothing.

"I'll take this up to your room," said Boss Veil, indicating her suitcase. "You'll be in the loft." He carried the suitcase up a narrow staircase.

"I'm Lizzie Parker," she announced awkwardly to the tall man.

"I'm Wilton," he responded in a monotone. "I help Boss Veil with the office work."

They said nothing else until Boss Veil returned down the stairs. "Up you go," he said. "Sleep well."

That was it? Lizzie had nothing to say except "Thank you" and "Goodnight."

As she walked upstairs, every step felt stranger than the one before. Where was she? Who were these men?

When she arrived at the top of the stairs, she saw that the loft was only slightly larger than the shed, but still it was a tremendous improvement. The walls and pitched ceiling were painted white. There was one small, square window. The bed looked not altogether unlike Red's coffin, except that it was slightly wider and stood off the floor. On it lay a blue patchwork quilt and a white pillow. Next to the bed sat a low bench with a gooseneck lamp, a large ceramic bowl, and two small towels.

She went to the bowl. It was filled with water. She dipped her fingers. Warm! She tasted it. Not salty! She sat on the bed, moistened one towel, and scrubbed her face, neck, and underarms.

Never mind that she didn't have soap. Never mind that she was sleeping in a house with two strange men. She had made it. Away from the loggers and the shed and the laundry—from the dirt and noise and failure—to a bowl of warm water. Boss Veil would telegram Esther. Lizzie was safe.

CHAPTER
SIX

"Father!" She felt like a wild animal. Fighting and scratching and yelling. Was she yelling aloud, or was she dreaming? He was there, in the dining room. He sat at the head of a long table. Behind him the china cabinet glowed with white china, and in front of him white sheets of paper glowed on the glossy dark wood. His white dress shirt was unbuttoned. His eyes were pink, in a way that made her think of blood.

Voices were rising from downstairs. Boss Veil and Wilton.

The loft was filling with light. She opened her eyes. She had to go down. She put on her blue-checkered dress with the drop waist. It was the last clean dress she had, but it felt silly with her filthy shoes. Her hair was so dirty she didn't want to touch it, but she made herself quickly brush it out and re-braid it. Blistered from the lye, her hands felt like balls of fever. She made herself smile.

Downstairs Boss Veil and Wilton were seated at the table sipping from mugs and studying paperwork. They didn't notice her at first, so she was able to look about the room. The rafters and wood floor were knotty, unpainted wood, but compared to the cookhouse, the place was a sanctuary. No profanity or tobacco spit. No shouts or leers. No arm wrestling or boot stomping. The kitchen could have been something for an embroidery sample. Pots and pans hung from the rafters, and lettuces, carrots, and bright purple plums were organized neatly by the sink. Out the large windows, framed by sunlit trees, the sky was bright blue. Dashes of light sparkled on the bay.

Boss Veil looked up. "Good morning, Miss Parker. How did you sleep?"

"Very well, thank you."

Wilton stood and pulled a chair back for her. "Toast is ready," he said in a voice just as flat as it had been the night before. "Would you like me to fry an egg?"

"Oh, no. Just toast is wonderful."

"Goodness, girl, what'd you do to your hands?" asked Boss Veil, pushing his face to see.

"Laundry," she said, dropping her hands to her lap.

"Laundry indeed." Boss Veil sat across from her, studying her, but said nothing. He looked like a fox. His nose was like a snout, and his small eyes were pressed deep back under his brow. "It's a shame that you ended up here. Your uncle's letter, the one to wave you off, must've gotten lost. The mail out here can be unreliable in the best of circumstances, and there were storms and fires last month that didn't help anything."

Lizzie thought of how many boats and trucks and crates and bags it had taken for her to arrive here. Of course the mail wouldn't be reliable.

"And it's doubly a shame that we don't know where your uncle has gone, either. Or, I suppose we do—I think he and your Aunt Louise are in California, visiting her family."

California? Was that how far they'd gone? Her chest filled with heat, then emptiness.

The boss continued, "I don't have a way of contacting him. Do you?"

"Me? No."

Boss Veil sucked something from one of his top teeth and licked the inside of his mouth. His lips were thin, nearly nonexistent. He finished his licking and swallowed. "Very well. There is an errand run to Mink Cove the day after tomorrow, and I will send a telegram to your sister on your behalf."

"Thank you!" Her heart lifted. A real plan. "How long do you think it will take for the money to arrive, once my sister sends it?"

Boss Veil looked to Wilton, who was working at the kitchen counter. "What do you think? A week? Two?"

"Depends on when the sister mails it. But that's about right. A week or two."

A week or two. Was that a long time or a short time? The calm in the men's voices made it seem that give or take a week, it didn't matter. But to Lizzie, two weeks versus one seemed an awful difference.

A huge splash sounded from the harbor. An explosion of water, as if something heavy had fallen off the dock.

Boss Veil scooted his chair back from the table. He lifted a pair of binoculars from a hook on the wall. "I should see about that," he said, less to Lizzie than to Wilton. Then he went outside to the deck. Through the windows, she could see him, pressing the binoculars to his eyes, looking out over the harbor, surveying his kingdom.

After a few minutes he returned inside and said, "They're just dunking clam buckets. But I ought to make sure they've secured everything properly. The tug will be by this afternoon to pick up this raft of logs."

"Very well," said Wilton.

To Lizzie, Boss Veil explained, "I can't trust these men to do things on their own. I ought to go straight to the prisons to recruit for next summer."

He laughed, but Lizzie wasn't sure whether he was joking. She thought back to the rowdy cookhouse. She was grateful to be in this clean kitchen. Boss Veil pushed his arms through his suit jacket and buttoned it over his shirt and tie. He checked a gold pocket watch and slid it back into its pocket. "I'll be back for a bourbon before supper," he announced. "Enjoy the day, Miss Lizzie."

Wilton went back to the dishes. Lizzie nibbled her toast and watched him. He scrubbed and rinsed and set all the items in a drying rack set on a yellow dishtowel. All of this was quite like a normal kitchen, except there was a row of other things, jars on a low shelf: yarn, nails, other workshop-type items her father would've known what to call. Wilton patted the pocket of his apron, took something out, and dropped it into a Folgers coffee can. As he stepped to do so, Lizzie heard a dragging noise. His right foot lagged behind the left. A limp.

"I got a piece of shrapnel in my foot during the war," he said without turning around, as if he could feel her stare. "Got infected, so they took everything off from below the knee."

She hated hearing about the war. Her civics teacher Mr. Samson had gone to France and told Lizzie's class about mustard gas. Lizzie's father had had poor eyesight and hadn't gone. "Otherwise I wouldn't have met your mother and had my beautiful daughters," he liked to say. Had liked to say.

There was a scratching at the door. First gentle, then fast. Lizzie remembered the cat that Boss Veil had kicked off the porch the night before. Wilton let the animal in. It meowed and rubbed Wilton's ankles. Wilton leaned down to scratch a white patch between its ears. The cat closed its eyes and tilted up its chin. Its chest was white, as well as its two hind paws.

"What's its name?" asked Lizzie.

"Tertius calls her Ratter because she hunts the rats—that's why he keeps her around—but I call her Kitty. But don't tell him. She's not supposed to be inside."

She meowed, and Wilton rubbed down her back and out to the end of her tail.

"What's that?" asked Lizzie. On the window seat, on a heap of books, was a basket. She craned her neck. Inside were knitting needles, a ball of yarn, and what appeared to be an attempt at a sock. The foot part was so small it would fit Robert, but the ankle opening was sized for an adult. The yarn was brown and stiff looking, like twine.

"Is that a sock?" she asked.

"Oh, that. The kitchen girl from last summer left it behind. I think it's beyond repair."

Lizzie picked up the basket. Nearly a stitch per row was dropped. Half the stitches were too tight, the other half too loose. "I think you'd just have to start all over. Do you want me to do it? I can knit."

"Go ahead," said Wilton. "In fact, take it upstairs with you. I need to do something that is *not* feeding a cat." He gave her a meaningful look.

"Of course," said Lizzie. She looked innocently around the room. "Because there aren't any cats here."

Upstairs, she heard a can open. A utensil mashed something into a bowl. The cat slurped and chomped. Lizzie could even hear her grooming after she was finished. The house was like a dollhouse. She could hear every noise. There was no door to her loft stairs. There were spaces between the floorboards.

She settled cross-legged on her bed and unwound the woebegone sock. To be fair, to make a sock was no simple thing. She only knew how because she and Mary had been knitting Christmas stockings to sell at the school bazaar for the past two years. Mary's mother had taught the girls, and Lizzie had memories of sitting on the carpet in front of the fire as Mary's mom helped them stitch on jingle bells and felt snowflakes.

After Lizzie's father had died, there was talk of her moving in with Mary's family. Mary's father's job at the university was stable, and they had a large house. The problem was that Mary's grandparents lived with them and were both in frail health.

"They have enough burdens," was how Esther had explained it.

Burden. That's what Lizzie was. A burden. A burden to be sent to Portland.

Lizzie had finished unraveling the sock, but her hands lay heavily in her lap. She forced herself to continue. Concentrate. How do you start a sock? Four needles— that was it. She needed to create a little square, and then knit a tube. She rummaged through the basket. Only three needles. No wonder this sock hadn't turned out.

Lizzie had packed her soon-to-be nephew's or niece's soakers in her suitcase, but those needles were too small. But perhaps, for just a prop needle, she could use two small needles in place of one large one. At least it was worth a try.

Lizzie unbuckled her suitcase. At the top was *Little Women*. Maybe she would read a chapter before she started knitting and then save another for after she'd made progress with the sock.

She opened the book, and by instinct, flipped to the inside back cover where she'd tucked the photograph of her family. But it wasn't there. She ran her fingers over the inside cover, as if she might be able to feel for it, then shook through the pages, riffling through each one. But there was no photo. She took everything out of her suitcase. Two dresses, one skirt, two blouses, one fresh pair of stockings, her blue sweater, and her nightdress.

She shook out the clothes and refolded them. She checked her yellow yarn and her coin purse. Nothing.

A cold trembling gathered in her. The photograph couldn't have gone missing. It just couldn't. It must've fallen out in the shed. That was all. Certainly no one would've stolen it. It had no value to anyone but her.

Oh, she should have been more careful. Maybe a mouse was using it for a toilet, or a crow was carrying it off for its nest right now. She had to find it. But . . . she didn't know where the shed was. When she had followed Boss Veil the evening before, she hadn't kept track of the route. She could ask Wilton, she supposed— he was still clattering away in the kitchen—but she didn't want to explain why. And, frankly, she was in no hurry to see the hideous shed again. She could wait until supper. She would find the photograph.

She allowed herself one chapter of *Little Women* and then proceeded with the sock. Her two-for-one needle device worked serviceably, and she was able to make good progress on the shaft of the sock. It would have to be tall, because the men's boots were so high, but the knitting went quickly because the yarn was so fat.

Every hour, as a reward, she allowed herself a new chapter, and by the time Boss Veil arrived home before supper, she realized the day had passed easily. Or, not as terribly as the day before.

"Miss Parker? Would you like a cocktail?" Boss Veil called.

"No, thank you."

"Do join us anyhow then."

She gathered her knitting and descended the stairs. Boss Veil looked tired but dignified, his clothes not caked in filth and pitch the way his crew members' were. He was sitting on the davenport, resting a tumbler on his belly. His eyes were half-closed.

"Wilton says you fixed a sock," he said, without opening his eyes.

"I'm almost done with one, but I still have to complete the foot and the toe."

Boss Veil opened his eyes, and timidly she handed him the sock. He rubbed the toe between his thumb and forefinger. "Looks like a sock to me," he said and passed it back.

"I'll be faster on the next one because I'll know how many stitches. This one I had to make up the pattern. In fact, there are a few places I think might not be just right. But—"

The boss waved his glass in her direction to say he didn't want to hear any more. The liquor was gone. The ice rattled in a bit of water. "It's fine," he said. "Just the right thing to keep you busy while we wait."

Boss Veil closed his eyes again. *We,* he'd said. While *we* wait. What was he waiting for?

CHAPTER SEVEN

"Do you know what happened to my uncle?"

Lizzie asked Red and Freddie this at dinner. After their cocktails, Boss Veil and Wilton had stayed back at the house, but Lizzie had followed the smell of chimney smoke and savory cooking and walked the path through the woods to the cookhouse. Now the cookhouse was filled with a sweaty din. It was nearly six o'clock, but the sky was still warm with summer light. The meal was discs of meat in brown gravy. Lizzie ate bread.

Red finished chewing. "He was supposed to invest money in the camp. He wanted to check out the business and give his boys a taste of the great outdoors at the same time. Romanticization of nature. That kind of thing."

Invest. There was that word again, from the newspaper's headline.

"Those boys," groaned Freddie. His hair was dark with sweat and raked sleekly back off his forehead. "One of them nicked his thumb on an ax, which he shouldn't have been playing with to start with, and wailed like he'd been stabbed in the gut."

"That's why they left?" asked Lizzie.

"No," said Red, cutting a piece of meat. "Your uncle decided not to invest. Or at least that's what I heard. The boss blamed it on your fancy aunt who didn't like being in the woods. Why are you wondering about your uncle?"

"Oh, I don't know." She wasn't after just one answer to one question—she wanted to know the whole thing. Why she was here. How things had gone so wrong. Because if she could figure it out, then maybe she could get home sooner. Or at least know that she would indeed go home at all. One day of knitting a sock alone was all right, but she wasn't sure how many more she could take.

"I have to say, I wouldn't want to work with the boss." Freddie grimaced. "He's a squirrelly son of a gun."

"But you do work with him," said Lizzie.

"I work *for* him. And not up close and personal. Most of us"—Freddie gestured around the dining hall—"don't see much of him. He barely ever goes into the woods. Mainly he oversees things down at the beach, making sure all the logs are counted up in his tally book before they get shipped off."

Lizzie thought of his fancy clothes and slippery shoes.

Red finished chewing. "He inherited the camp from his father. Or rather, he didn't inherit the sawmill. That went to his brother, and the boss hasn't gotten over it. I just think the father wanted to be rid of ole Tertius."

"I say you mind your own business," said Freddie to Lizzie. "Just think about getting paid, and that's it."

Lizzie thought of the hundred dollars and Portland. She wasn't getting paid anything. She was wasting money, traveling up here only to go home again, immediately if she could. A weight descended on her, then a light fluttery panic. She had so many questions and no answers at all.

Lizzie didn't ask anything else for the rest of dinner. Afterward, as the plates were being cleared, Freddie and another man stayed behind with a deck of cards. The man was middle-aged but neither gray-haired nor bald. His suspenders were off his shoulders and dangled over the side of the bench.

She wondered what they were playing. It looked like poker. Her father had played cards with her. It was the only thing they did together after supper. Poker was her favorite, but they also played rummy and double solitaire. Before Robert was born, Thomas and Esther would join for bridge. Although Esther was better than Lizzie at pretty much everything, Lizzie could usually beat her at cards.

"Do you play?" asked Freddie.

"Not really," she answered, embarrassed that he'd noticed her staring.

"Five-card draw? You could be our third."

"I should go back and do some knitting."

Or look for her photo. She'd need to ask someone where the shed was, but she was terrible with directions. Someone might need to walk her there. And then she'd have to explain about the photograph, and they'd have to wait while she looked. She sighed. She didn't want to do any of that. Maybe the photograph could wait. It would be better to look in the daylight anyway.

"Come on," said Freddie. "Knitting's for girls." He winked. Winked! She didn't know what to do. On the one hand, she didn't want to embarrass herself at cards. On the other hand, there was Freddie. Handsome Freddie with his unbuttoned shirt and tan arms. Grinning at her from across the table.

"Got money?" asked the mustached man gruffly.

Ha! She wanted to laugh aloud. But . . . there was Freddie, still smiling. "One hand," he said.

"Fine." She didn't have enough to go home anyway, so a nickel or two wouldn't matter one way or another.

"Swell," said Freddie. "Let the games begin."

She took her seat down at their end of the table.

"This is Wally," Freddie said, nodding to the mustached man. He—Wally—grunted by way of greeting, and Lizzie had to prevent herself from laughing out loud. With his round face and upside-down *U* mustache, he looked just like a walrus.

"Pleased to meet you," she said. "Should I get my coin purse? It's back at Boss Veil's house."

"We'll use matchsticks for now," said Freddie. "Then cash them out at the end of the night. Each one's a dime."

He slid a small heap across the table. It was a lot of money. It was *real* money. At home, they played just for fun. How much could she afford to lose? She had three dollars in her coin purse. She could risk twenty cents. Thirty tops.

Freddie shuffled. Wally picked his teeth with a toothpick.

Lizzie stacked her matches into a pyramid. The table had been wiped down—Gladys kept a tidy cookhouse—yet it was still filthy. Years, or decades, of grime had built up on it like wax. There were streaks of black, deep into the grain of the wood, from which seemed to rise the odors of a million dinners of grease and ketchup.

She and her father had played at the polished mahogany dining room table. The cards had slid across it so smoothly that sometimes, when being dealt, they'd slide clear across the table and onto the carpet. A beautiful red carpet with a green trellis pattern. Where was that carpet now? It must have been sold. All of the furniture was sold. Thomas had done it. "Taken care of it," was how Esther had put it. "And still it's not enough money. Not even close."

Freddie finished shuffling. Wally cut the deck, and Freddie dealt. His fingers were stained yellow from swirling snoose. Dirt was packed under his fingernails and into the skin around the nails. Wally's fingers were just the same.

Lizzie's father's hands had been clean. Tidy square nails, pale freckled skin, not even very much hair. She remembered his gold wristwatch clinking against the edge of the table.

"Lizzie? Do you want to pick up your cards?"

She fanned out the cards, which were smudged and creased at the corners. A pair of threes, a seven, a nine and a ten. She had to remind herself about the game. The basic idea was that, to win, she had to have cards that matched or were all in a row. Her pair of threes was good but not fantastic.

Freddie was waiting on her to bet. She brought her attention back to the game. Wally had bet three matches, she counted. Thirty cents. Her hand wasn't good enough for her to want to risk that much, so she folded.

Freddie put in three matches to meet Wally's. His face was blank. Pretty good. She remembered what her dad had said about a poker face: less is more.

Freddie and Wally each traded in two cards. Freddie's face stayed the same, but Wally's broke into a grin. He slid five matches into the pot.

"No way," groaned Freddie, folding.

Wally laughed and raked all the matches toward him. What did he have in his hand? Had he bluffed? She waited for him to show what he had in his hand, but instead he shuffled his cards back into the deck. She remembered that the winner didn't have to show his cards unless another player called his bet. That was the official rule. With her family, the winner had always shown their cards for fun.

But this, now, wasn't fun. This was money. And she didn't have any to waste.

She was about to excuse herself, but Wally was sliding the deck across the table toward her. "Cut."

Against her will she reached for them. She'd forgotten how good it felt, the sense that something better was just around the corner. She set aside the top half of the deck, then laid the bottom half on top. She slid the stack back to Wally.

Wally dealt. She picked up her cards and organized them. A good hand. Or, not a bad one. Two queens, a three, a five and a nine. She tried to hide her pleasure, but it didn't matter. Freddie and Wally were just looking at each other.

Aha. Being invisible might be useful.

Freddie pushed two matchsticks into the pot. Wally did the same but raised him another matchstick. He gave Freddie a look of satisfaction, as if to say, "I'll show you."

Now her turn. She tried to stay calm. Think it through, that's what her father would have said. She imagined his voice in her head. Do you think you have a better hand than these jokers?

Maybe. And it's only thirty cents, and there's a chance I could draw a queen. . . . She slid her three matches into the pot.

Freddie and Wally raised their eyebrows at her.

"Well, well, well, little lady," said Wally. She couldn't tell if he was mocking her, or enjoying the competition. But the surprise in his voice irritated her. She was sitting there playing, wasn't she? Why wouldn't she bet?

Freddie laughed good-naturedly. "What the hell." He pushed in another match. They were all even. Now time to trade in their cards.

Wally went first. He traded in three of his five cards. That probably meant he had a pair and three bad cards. That was a good sign—for her. He smiled as he looked at his new cards. Maybe he had gotten good ones. That was possible.

Now Lizzie's turn. She passed in her three low cards. Please get another queen, she thought. Please, please, please. Wally's yellow fingers slid the new cards back to her. And . . . yes! A queen. So now she had three queens. Three of a kind was good, and three queens was extra good. Her two other cards, a nine and a jack, were also high.

Calm down, she told herself. Don't smile.

Freddie's turn. He traded in three cards. He looked at the new ones thoughtfully, then pushed in three matches.

Wally smirked at Lizzie. It was his turn to bet. He nodded at her slowly, sizing her up. Then he looked down at his hand and twisted his mouth to the side, thinking, and his mustache twitched. He wasn't going to fold, she could tell. But how much was he going to bet?

With his stubby index finger, he counted out matches. One . . . two, to match Freddie . . . three . . . then four . . . five . . . six . . . seven! Seventy cents? If she matched his bet, combined with the thirty cents she'd already bet, she'd be out a dollar. That was a third of the money she had at camp. The words "I fold" were almost out of her mouth when Wally said, "Did your daddy send you here with enough money for that?"

Something hot flared in her. *If he only knew.*

Wally noticed her pause. "Oh, so you're thinking about a bet?" he asked. His voice was a little louder than normal.

Louder. His voice was too loud. That's what her father said was a "tell," the thing that gives away a bluffer. Esther always talked loudly, but it was almost comical the way her voice rose with a bad hand.

Wally had traded in three cards, Lizzie remembered. What were the chances he had anything as good as three queens with two other high cards? Barely any chance at all. With a gulp of air, she pushed in seven matchsticks. And added another. But as soon as she let them go, her confidence vanished. She could lose. But there was no taking the matches back now.

Freddie said, "Too much for me," and folded his hand.

Wally studied the pot, which was now two dollars and seventy cents, counting Freddie's ante. She counted the money in her head. She'd put in a dollar and ten cents. She could hardly believe it. How could she have risked that much? But if she won, she'd win over a dollar and a half. Added to the two dollars and fifteen cents she already had, it would be enough to get her home. She did the math again. The boat, the trolley, the train. It would be enough. She wanted to jump out of her skin.

Wally did the thing with his mouth again, twitching one side of his mustache, but he kept his eyelids lowered.

"Fold," he said flatly and set his cards facedown on the table.

"Really? I won?" She was too excited to put down her cards. She was going home. She could hardly believe it.

Freddie was grinning. "Well done, Miss Lizzie." He motioned for her cards, and she passed them in. "Another round?"

"I should quit while I'm ahead," she said. She hoped she didn't sound boastful. She honestly meant that she could very well lose everything in the next round. Also, now that the nervousness had drained from her body, she was nearly limp with exhaustion.

Home. She was going home. Maybe not tomorrow, but whenever the next boat left for Vancouver. And then all this would be over.

"Fine then. Let's cash you out."

Wally and Freddie dug into their pockets and exchanged the match sticks for coins.

"Thank you," she said, enjoying the coins' weight in her hands.

"You won't be thanking us next time," said Wally. His voice was gruff, but maybe she also heard a bit of playfulness? She was flattered that he wanted her to play again. But she needed to keep her money so that she could leave—maybe even soon.

She said goodnight to Freddie and Wally, and trotted up the path to Boss Veil's house. The sun was low on the water but had not yet set. Golden light glowed on the rocks and trees, warmed the spongy soil, yet also carried in a hint of cold. The first finger of night.

She clutched the money in her palm inside the pocket of her skirt. She was on her way home.

She climbed the porch, and Boss Veil opened the door. His jacket was off, and he wore only his vest. His shirt was unbuttoned at the collar, and she could see the top of his undershirt. A tumbler of liquor—she could smell its vapor—clinked in his right hand. A moist flush crept up his neck and spread over his nose and cheeks and ears. His bleary eyes met hers. "Where have you been?"

"I was playing poker. I made enough money to pay my way home." She didn't suppress her grin. She didn't want to seem proud, but she assumed that Boss Veil would share in her pleasure.

But he didn't seem pleased. At all. His brow furrowed over his fox eyes, and he clenched his jaw. "Poker?"

"Yes," she said. What had she done wrong?

To her relief, Wilton arrived at the door. "Come in," he said. "You're bringing in the bugs. Now what's going on?"

"I won at poker." She showed them the coins. "Now I have enough to go home."

"That is vulgar!" exclaimed Boss Veil, turning from the money in disgust. "How do you know how to play poker? You are a *little girl*. And aren't you a pauper? I thought you didn't have any money. And now you're going around like you're at a casino?"

"Tertius," said Wilton. He put a long-fingered hand on Boss Veil's shoulder.

Boss Veil was quiet. Finally he said, "We will send you on the next trip to Vancouver. You can take the train from there."

"When will that be?"

Anger flared again in Boss Veil's eyes. His jaw flexed to hold back rage. She'd been bold to speak again.

Wilton broke in. "Sunday, so the day after tomorrow."

Sunday. That was nearly now. Only one more day. She felt she could get air again. Now all she wanted was to be alone.

Upstairs, she collapsed onto her bed and listened to the men below. Boss Veil spoke loudly—"money," "go home"—but Wilton shushed him. He spoke soothingly, and soon the men quieted and readied for bed.

Lizzie's body was heavy and stiff. She felt unable to undress. What was going on? Boss Veil should've been glad she was going home, but he'd been disgusted. Maybe he was right. She was vulgar. A penniless girl at a casino.

But a girl who'd won. She snapped the money into her coin purse. She didn't undress. She kept the purse in her hand and brought it under the covers with her. She listened to the waves rattle the dock, the boats squeak in their moorings, and the lines slap against the sailboat's mast. All night her fingers wrapped around her purse and pressed it to her chest as if it were a second heart.

CHAPTER EIGHT

Lizzie didn't dream of poker but felt it. Her sleep was light and nervous. When the sounds of Wilton's clanging on the stove woke her, she didn't want to go downstairs. Her body and eyelids were heavy, her pillow warm in the sunshine that slanted through the window.

What a faraway time it had been at Esther's house, when she'd taken afternoon naps. It was an indulgence Esther had allowed after she'd become tired due to pregnancy. On weekends, during Robert's afternoon nap, she and Lizzie would doze too. Esther and Robert would nap in the bedroom, and Lizzie would doze on the davenport without assembling her full bed, just resting her head on the pansy-pattern needlepoint pillow with the purple velvet backing. She could smell it now. The hay bale of the needlepoint, the slightly perfumed velvet. The friendly noise of passing automobiles, or neighborhood children, or Thomas walking up the porch with groceries.

She didn't love living with Esther and Thomas, but it was familiar and safe and clean. She didn't want to go to Portland.

She wanted to cry. She wanted to squint up her eyes and face and whole body, and hide under her blanket and never come out. She wanted to say: I quit. No, more than that. I quit having gone to camp in the first place. I quit being an orphan. I quit the whole thing. I want to go back in time and erase it all.

No one called for her to wake up. She listened to Wilton and the boss have breakfast, and then they left. The house was quiet. She went downstairs. Fire crackled in the wood stove, and a pot of hot water steamed on the stovetop. A note on the kitchen table said, *I'll be doing inventory at the commissary until lunch. Wilton.*

Lizzie's stomach rumbled for breakfast, but she also needed to use the privy. She walked to the privy by the cookhouse, which was a small one, off-limits to the loggers and reserved for Boss Veil, Wilton, and Gladys. And, for the time being, Lizzie. She did her business quickly but lingered on the walk back. Smoke from the cookhouse faded into gray mist. Wood chips and needles were soft under her shoes. Perfumes of fish and rock drifted up from the beach. The air was cool but not cold. A few bits of sun fell through branches and landed, like petals, on moss.

Tomorrow she was going to leave. But then what? She had no job. Would she help Esther cook and clean for the boarders? Would she sleep in the bedroom with Esther and Thomas and the babies? Imagine a newborn, screaming all night. Or Esther could send her straight to Portland. And what would she do there while she waited for school to start? She imagined herself trapped in a bedroom, shades drawn, lying on a bed and staring at the ceiling.

She thought of Red's work on the railroad and felt envy, then foolishness. She couldn't do that. She didn't even want to.

In the loft, she packed her things. Not that there was much to pack, but she wanted to be ready. She wiped out dirt and tree needles from her suitcase, folded her clothes, and on the low bench next to the water basin, set out a clean, but wrinkled, blouse and skirt and the remaining pair of still-intact stockings for the next day's journey.

She couldn't forget her coin purse, so she set it front and center atop the dress. But as she handled it, it didn't feel full. It was light. Her heart started the thrum. She held her breath and undid the clasp.

Empty.

She opened the purse wider, swept the interior with her index finger. Just fabric and threads. *Where was the money?*

She hadn't lost it. Impossible. She'd had the purse there in her room the whole time. She remembered clear as day snapping the money inside. She'd thought of little else since last night. Someone must've stolen it. There was no other explanation. Someone must've known she'd left for the privy, snuck in, and found it.

Her chest felt like it was being pressed shut. She couldn't get enough air. She sat on the floor.

Was it Wally? His long mustache and brown teeth, his fat hands and forearms as big as three of hers. She should've known better than to win at poker. But he hadn't seemed that angry. In fact, he'd seemed somewhat friendly by the end.

It could be anyone. All of the men were poor. All of the men wanted money. She thought of their rowdy jokes and crude laughter. Even Red, who was kind to her, was a little crazy. She thought of Olavfur with his long ax and angry warnings. And Freddie. She had beaten him at poker too. But theft seemed beyond him. She pictured his cute puppy dog face when he'd asked her to play.

Or could it be Wilton—or Boss Veil? He'd been so angry the night before. He and Wilton had the chance, right here in this house. But they didn't need the money. They were the richest men at the camp.

She was too upset to cry. Too angry. She needed to do something. She would go downstairs. Alone, in the house, and just *see*. She'd say she was looking for breakfast if Boss Veil or Wilton returned. That would seem innocent enough.

She'd never been alone in the house before. It felt quiet and clean and big. She looked around. The fireplace, davenport, and dining table sat large and innocent. Her attention was drawn to the kitchen, to the canister of spatulas and wooden spoons, to the rows of cans and containers. She pictured Wilton working at the sink with his long, busy arms. Then she saw the Folgers coffee can. She remembered Wilton taking something out of his apron pocket and dropping it in the can.

The shelf was high. Quickly, she scooted over a chair, climbed up, and reached her hand into the can. She had to fumble around until she found a small metal object. Before she brought it down to look, she could tell what it was. A key.

Lizzie stepped off the chair and held the key in her palm. It was modern and shiny, which made her think that it opened the door of the house, by far the most up-to-date building at camp. It must be a house key then. That was all. She should put it right back.

But then she thought of the door at the bottom of the stairs to the loft. She had always assumed it was a closet, or a pantry, and perhaps it was—but was it *locked*?

Lizzie's blood started to pump more quickly, and she felt heat on her skin. She quieted her breathing and listened. No footsteps outside. Wilton would be gone awhile. The commissary was full of merchandise, and he was a slow walker. And it would only take a moment to try the key.

She pushed her chair back under the table, gingerly, as if someone might hear, even though she was alone. She peered around the room too, as if someone could be hiding. With a shiver, she thought of whomever had stolen her money. His presence, like a ghost, seemed to have entered the room. She rushed to the closet door. She wanted to get her experiment over with.

The key slid into the lock and turned.

The room wasn't a closet or a pantry, but a small office. A capsule from the modern world. Oversized calendars and maps were tacked onto the walls. A black typewriter sat on the desk. Next to it, small sheets of paper were jammed on a metal spike, and a stack of mail rested in a low, wire basket. At the top of the stack was an envelope that said *To: Mr. Andrew Parker*. Below it, *Parker Investment Company* at an address in Vancouver.

She read it again to be sure. Mr. Andrew Parker. Her uncle. The writing seemed fresh. The letter was on the top of this stack. But, if her uncle had left weeks ago, what did Boss Veil have to say to him now? And wasn't he in California?

She glanced over her shoulder. No one. She listened to the house. Nothing. She lifted the envelope. It was sealed, and it was heavier than the average letter. She tipped it vertically. Something slid downward in it. A card or ticket.

She scanned the desk for a letter opener. Maybe she could open the envelope and seal it back up. But that would be hard, and plus, she didn't see a letter opener. But there was a small jar of glue.

Glue—that was it. She could steam open the envelope and reseal it. She thought of the pot of water on the stove. But she had never steamed open a letter. She'd only read of it in books. And what if she messed up? Or she was caught?

She looked again at the letter. Maybe she should just put it back where she'd found it. It wasn't her business. Who knew what Boss Veil had to say to her uncle? It was probably just some last small piece of business. Could be perfectly ordinary.

Or not.

She had to act fast. If Wilton was doing inventory at the commissary, it wouldn't last all day. She scanned the desk once more for a letter opener, and her eye caught again on the glue. She'd better take it with her, to seal the letter back up. She dropped the small jar, which was sticky at the cap, into the pocket of her skirt.

In the kitchen, the pot on the stove was still so hot that she had to use an oven mitt to lift the lid. She did that with one hand, and with the other she waved the envelope over the steam. But it was too much, and the paper started to warp. The ink ran. She was ruining the letter! She clattered the lid shut, set the envelope on the counter, and dabbed the writing with the hem of her skirt. Had someone come in just then, they'd have seen her underpants, but she didn't care. She carefully blotted the envelope, dabbing around the rims of each letter, and by the time she'd finished, only a few looked slightly blurred. If Boss Veil or Wilton examined them closely, they might notice, but not at a normal distance, especially once the envelope was jumbled in with others. She'd have to hope.

The glue was loose, but she still needed something to shimmy open the envelope. A dinner knife would do the job. The first drawer she opened held the silverware.

As she grabbed a knife, she heard thumps on the stairs. Heavy and lopsided. Wilton.

Lizzie's body froze. She looked at her hand, holding the envelope. No time to put it back in the office. But what to do with it? It was too big for her pocket, so she tucked it into the waistband of her underwear and tucked her blouse into her skirt so the envelope didn't show, or at least she hoped it didn't. The paper, still damp yet sharp at the edges, was uncomfortable against her skin.

The glue! She swiped it off the counter and hid it in her pocket. She began to drop the knife into her pocket too but heard it clank against the jar of glue.

So she kept it in her grip, and when Wilton entered the kitchen, she was holding out the knife as if ready for an attack.

"Are you all right?" asked Wilton. He was a bit out of breath, and sweat dotted his skin. His face was the most expressive she'd seen it. He appeared surprised, even concerned.

"Yes," stammered Lizzie, but then her throat clamped shut. She was certain the letter was going to slip to the floor, or Wilton was going to ask about the bulge in her pocket or notice the ink on the hem of her skirt.

She had to say something. The longer she stood there like an idiot, the guiltier she'd seem. She looked again at the knife in her hand.

"Knife pleats! I'm making them on the socks, and I needed a knife. I'm sorry I didn't ask you. I should've asked." All this was a lie. She had never made knife pleats. She wasn't even sure what they were. All she knew was the name. And she was nearly certain she didn't need a knife to make them.

Wilton looked at her skeptically and said nothing. Maybe *he* knew about knife pleats. He'd been saving the socks to fix them, after all. Maybe he was an accomplished knitter. Maybe she should try another lie.

But before she could think of something else, Wilton said, "Very well. Take what you need." His voice was light and measured, to tell her that he knew something odd was going on.

She thanked him and walked in tiny steps up to the loft, careful not to let the envelope fall from her skirt. Upstairs she perched on the edge of her bed, listening to Wilton. Would he reach for the coffee can? Go into the office? Notice the missing letter? Soon, though, she heard him run the faucet and begin to chop something.

She looked at the letter. Seeing her uncle's name again made her stomach roll. What if she didn't want to know what was inside? No. She needed to know. She'd come this far.

With tiny sawing motions, she pushed the knife along underneath the flap of the envelope and managed to open it without tearing the paper. Phew, she sighed. At least that worked. She lifted out the letter, unfolded it, and there—plain as day—was the photograph. *Her* photograph. The one she'd lost. Her father, mother, sister, and herself. She flipped it over. There, in her father's faded writing, on the left-hand corner, *My loves. 1919.*

Her hands began to tremble. Boss Veil had stolen her photograph. She hadn't lost it. But why? The floor felt as if it were tilting under her, as if she were on a boat. She didn't want to read the letter but knew she had to.

Send the money if you want the girl. Accidents are easy to explain in the woods.

Lizzie threw the letter on her bed as if it were going to bite her. Her skin went cold. Money . . . girl . . . accidents.

Her pulse was so fast she felt she might shake herself out of her skin. This couldn't be true. She looked at the letter again. "Send money" and "accidents" meant her uncle needed to pay, or she could be hurt. Or die. She was being held for ransom. Her little room was not a bedroom but a cell. Its sweet blue quilt was a joke. Boss Veil and Wilton weren't her saviors but her captors. They must've stolen her poker money because they didn't want her to leave. And they stole the photograph to show to Uncle Andrew to prove she was at the camp. She pictured Wilton's pale, long fingers rifling through her underwear and soiled stockings.

While we wait—that's what the boss had said on her first night. And he hadn't acted surprised to see her. Boss Veil *wanted* her here alone. And her uncle wasn't in California. That was a lie too. A sick joke. If she hadn't found the letter, she would've never known. Until . . . *Accidents are easy to explain in the woods.*

She looked to her little window. It only opened an inch. But even if she could escape this house, she could not go far. What would she do? Hide in the woods? Swim?

"Miss Parker?" called Wilton from downstairs. "Do you want the hot water?"

Hot water. He knew about the steam, and her opening the letter. Oh no. Oh no, oh no, oh no.

"Miss Parker? You can wash your hair if you like. I have shampoo and a towel."

Lizzie exhaled. So it wasn't about the envelope. But what if it was a trick, just a way to get her downstairs? Well, it *was* a trick—it was *all* a trick. And the only thing to do, for now, was play along.

The office key, letter, and photograph still lay on the bed. She smoothed out the envelope, which had warped some with the steam, and pressed it into *Little Women*. Then she tucked the book, along with the key, under her pillow.

Downstairs, Wilton was holding a folded towel, a measuring cup, and a bottle of shampoo. His face was calm and pleasant. Or cold and calculating. Maybe he didn't know that Boss Veil was holding her for ransom. Or maybe he had devised the whole scheme himself.

"I set the water out on the porch already. And I'll give you some privacy. I'm headed back to the commissary."

After he'd disappeared down the path, she replaced the letter, locked the office door, dropped the key back into the coffee can, and sat on the porch.

Her uncle would pay the ransom. He and Aunt Louise were rich. Or maybe he'd show the ransom letter to the police. They would come together to Dark Water Bay and throw Boss Veil in jail. She wouldn't just be left here forever—would she?

A coldness prickled on her skin. She made herself put her fingertips in the water, and then her whole hands. She rested them there. The water felt good. Her breathing slowed. She felt weight and heat in her hands, her pulse running through them. That was it: she was alive. That was the whole point of being a hostage. Boss Veil didn't want to kill her. To get his money, he needed to keep her alive. For how long, she didn't know, but she could wait.

It had been days since she'd used soap. First she washed her face and hands, then she wrapped the towel around her neck to keep her sweater dry, unbraided her hair, and wet it by scooping up the water with the measuring cup. She had to lean her head over the side of the porch to let off the water. There was barely enough water for a full shampoo and lather of her face and neck. How much easier it would be, she thought, if her hair were short. But no matter. She added the shampoo, then scrubbed her scalp with her fingers for a long, long time. She closed her eyes and breathed slowly. How good it felt to have the blood tingling under her scalp. Her body, her skin, the water, and the trees were alive.

CHAPTER NINE

"I'd do a good job," said Freddie, taking off his cap and setting it beside his dinner plate. He pushed his dark hair off his brow. "I'm good at climbing. I'd make a good assistant."

"You're doing a good job as a punk," said Red, reaching for a pitcher of water. "Punking's fine work."

Lizzie sat with Red and Freddie at the dinner table. She heard their words, but they floated by at a distance. All the energy from discovering the letter was gone. That afternoon, after her shampoo, as she'd sat knitting cross-legged on her bed and letting her hair dry in the light through her small window, she'd barely turned the heel of one sock.

Captive. She was Boss Veil's captive.

At dinner, to her relief, Wilton announced that he and Boss Veil would, again, eat by themselves. Would Lizzie mind setting a good example for the criminals? Wilton had asked, in his flat humor. *I hate you*, she'd thought. *I know how bad you are.* But she'd said nothing.

She said nothing now, either. She looked around the room at the loggers. At hands so calloused and dirty that even washed skin look stained. At lips rimmed in black tobacco. At missing teeth and scarred cheeks. At arms so dense with muscles they were as thick around as three or four or five of her own arms.

Did the men know about Boss Veil's scheme? Did Red and Freddie know? Were they helping Boss Veil keep an eye on her?

She watched them. White hairs dangled from Red's nose. Freddie prattled on about wanting a new job. She thought of Red's novels and coffin. Boss Veil wouldn't involve him with a kidnapping plan. Red wouldn't go along with anyone's nonsense unless it was his own. Freddie was too young. Boss Veil wouldn't trust him with a secret.

Boss Veil wouldn't want anyone to know. It would only increase the risk of her finding out. And he might have to split the ransom money. Besides, he needed no help keeping her captive. She was surrounded by woods and water. The whole camp was her cell.

"Are you all right?" asked Red. He frowned at her. His blue eyes flickered with concern. "You aren't eating. Here, it's good." He passed the platter of brown discs in brown sauce and a concoction of onion and pale pink nuggets. "Beef tongue and pigs' feet salad."

"No, thank you," said Lizzie. She didn't even want water, but she didn't protest as Red poured some into her specked tin mug. She forced herself to take a sip.

"I could learn to climb in an hour," said Freddie.

Red looked at him wearily. "You're just going to have to wait till someone loses his ear."

Lizzie nearly spat out her water. "An ear?"

Red pointed to a pair of boots dangling from a nail by the cookhouse door. They were small, for men's boots, and had red laces. "Skunky Abe. He got an ax to the side of his head. Too bad he was such a tiny little fella. Otherwise someone'd be using the boots."

"He didn't die," Freddie added. "Just lost the ear. But that was lucky, really. Any deeper of a slice and he would've died in the boat. I helped carry him down the hill. He was bleeding so much all down his neck"— Freddie dragged his hand down his own neck to show— "that he soaked through his whole shirt and even onto his pants. He bled onto me, too, and Gladys had to scrub my clothes all the next day. But by some miracle, he made it to the hospital and survived."

"But without an ear," said Red, chewing.

Freddie nodded. "The poor guy carried the ear into the hospital in his pocket. I imagine they tossed it out, though. What were they going to do, sew it back on?"

Accidents are easy to explain in the woods. Maybe Boss Veil wasn't just threatening to kill her. Maybe he would cut off some part of her body and mail it to her uncle, saying if he didn't send the money, something worse would happen. Like something out of a true crime book. Her stomach climbed up in her throat. She looked at the chopped-up pigs feet and nearly threw up into her napkin.

"What if someone does something like that on purpose?" she asked. "Hurts another man? Are there police around here?"

As she heard the question come out of her mouth, she understood how foolish it was. There were no roads. She'd seen no people at all, besides members of the camp.

Red cocked his head and peered at her even more curiously than he had before. "Police? I think we've got enough criminals here that we police ourselves."

"I think I'm the only fella in this whole place who hasn't committed a crime," said Freddie.

"Yet," winked Red.

She didn't want them to joke. She was serious. She felt tears gathering but swallowed them back. She took a few deep breaths to make sure she wouldn't cry, then asked, "How long will mail take to reach Vancouver?"

"Aren't you sending the letter to your sister in Seattle?" asked Red.

"Oh, um, yes," she stammered, trying to think of a lie. She didn't want them to know about the ransom. That would only make things worse. "But Boss Veil said something about mailing it through Vancouver."

"Well, if the letter were delivered to the ferry at Powell River, then it could take just a few days. But if it's sent through Mink Cove—"

"The mail is unreliable up here, I know."

For the rest of the meal, Freddie pestered Red about becoming the climber's assistant, whatever that meant. Afterward, Red went to the commissary to buy tobacco, and Freddie asked if she wanted to play poker again. "Pretty please? I'll only try to beat you a tiny bit."

"No, thanks. I'll quit while I'm ahead."

"Suit yourself." Freddie pouted. Her heart sank. She did want to play—and to be near Freddie—very much. But she didn't have any money to bet with since her previous night's winnings had been stolen, and, more importantly, she didn't want to anger Boss Veil again. Especially knowing what she did now.

"Good night, then," she said, and started to walk to Boss Veil's house. She passed the loggers' cabins. Some men sat on the porch cleaning boots. Two men played a checkers game set up on a big stump. One man darned a sock. Another played the harmonica. A few men waved. No one said anything. She felt conspicuous yet invisible, which was a terrible way to feel.

As she neared Boss Veil's house, she slowed. She didn't want to go in. Even though she wasn't worried Boss Veil or Wilton would hurt her—at least not yet— she didn't want to be near them.

Without really deciding, she walked in a direction she'd never been. Some trees had been cut away. Low bushes were pruned back haphazardly. She felt reckless, but she decided that if Boss Veil or Wilton found her or asked where she'd been, she'd say she'd gotten lost looking for the privy.

Heat pumped into her legs. Her lungs filled with cool air. The breeze lifted the smells of grease and tobacco from the cookhouse off of her. A bush caught on her stockings. She wished she had trousers and tall socks and boots like the men's. She wished she had a tarpaulin, and a lantern, and a canteen, and food. She could keep walking, far into the woods, away from Boss Veil. Build a fire. Listen for bears.

Her father used to tell her about camping in the Olympic Mountains, across Puget Sound from Seattle. His father, her grandfather, would pack eggs and butter on a mule. That's all she remembered. She didn't care about the woods back then. And her father didn't know about *these* woods. Dark Water Bay. This wasn't a place for a summer hike. Her father wouldn't know what to do here any better than she did.

The semi-path descended steeply. She had to step carefully and lean to hold on to tree trunks. Rocks jutted through the soil. The woods ended, and she was at a beach. It was small, less than a third the length of the main beach, and covered with logs. Not fresh logs but dead ones. Dozens and dozens, stacked as high on the beach as the tide could push them. They must have been collecting there for ages. They were as dry and cracked as bones.

But the sunset, the sunset was alive. Without the dock and the men and the boats, there was nothing but water and the few silhouetted islands far in the distance. Light radiated from the horizon in stripes. Orange, blue, and silver. The water was glass. The water was on fire.

It was beautiful. More beautiful than anything she could imagine. She wanted to cry. Cry because there was nothing to *do* with the beauty except let it hit her. She thought about the water and the rocks, cold and lasting forever, and she knew how small she was. She was nothing at all. No one wanted her except for Boss Veil, and he only wanted to replace her with money.

Something rustled behind her. Something in the woods.

An animal? Boss Veil? Had he noticed the envelope had been opened? Yes—the sounds were from a person. Branches thwacked against legs, and small things cracked under feet. A faint voice hummed. It was distracted, almost whistling. She saw a glimpse of snowy hair.

"Red?"

"Who's that?" Red stepped out of the woods. He stopped and looked at her in surprise. "What are you doing out here?"

"Watching the sunset?"

"A bit off the beaten path, I must say. This is my secret hiding place."

"What are you hiding?"

"Myself, I suppose. But I'll let you stay. Here, sit."

He gestured to one of the enormous bone-looking logs. They had to cross a few smaller logs, and their dry wood crumbled under her shoes. Seaweedy bog slurped below. She was relieved to finally sit, but splinters scratched the backs of her thighs. Although Red's pants were fraying at the knees, their canvas looked ten times as thick as the silly poplin of her dress. She propped her Oxfords on the log in front of them, a bit lower as if it had been designed to be a footrest. She noticed a smear of blood where the bush had snagged her stockings. She thought of wiping it away, but then decided not to bother. No one cared how she looked.

Red pulled aside one of his suspenders and fumbled in his breast pocket. She knew even before he withdrew it: a cigarette. Then, from his trouser pocket, a match, which he struck on the edge of the sole of his boot. After he lit his cigarette and had waved out the match in the wind, he balanced the match on his knee as its smoke curled into the air.

"Don't want to light the beach on fire," he said.

"Are there fires up here?" She remembered Boss Veil and Wilton saying something about a fire.

"Usually a couple per summer, in this whole area. Dark Water Bay hasn't had one in a long time, though."

"How do the fires start?"

"Oh, plenty of ways. Idiots like me who smoke on a dried-out log, or tramps who cook in the woods, or good old-fashioned lightning."

"Are there people to put out the fires, like firemen?"

"Goodness, my girl. What do you think?" He paused to let her examine the thick, emerald forest and calm, glassy bay. A fish jumped.

"I guess not," she said, forcing a chuckle. No one—truly no one—was going to find her.

Red propped his elbow on his knee, dangled the cigarette over his boot, then offered it in her direction. She shook her head no. Luckily there was a breeze that was carrying the smoke away from her eyes. A chunk of ash and ember floated off the tip of the cigarette, and they watched as it faded from orange to gray on the log. The ash was the same color as the powdery wood.

"Where's all this worrying coming from?" Red asked. "You asked about police at supper, and now a fire? What's going on?"

I'm a captive at a logging camp in the middle of nowhere, that's what's going on, thought Lizzie. But was she going to tell Red? She hadn't been expecting him to ask. She hadn't been expecting any of this. Oh, how uncertain she was. That was what made her cry now. That she just didn't know what to *do*. She sniffled and wiped away tears with the side of her hand. She looked away, down the beach. The sun had nearly set. The orange light had burned out, leaving only gray. The forest was growing black, taking in its secrets for the night.

"Is it Boss Veil?" asked Red. "Is he hurting you?"

"Hurting me?"

"I mean, in that house. Is that what's going on?"

He stared at her fiercely. He wasn't going to say anything more, but she knew suddenly what he meant.

"No. It's nothing like that. It's just . . ."

She looked at Red, his delicate body, nearly as small as her own, perched just the right distance away. Not too close, not too far. Asking the right questions. She wanted to tell him something. Something small, to see what he'd say.

"I found a letter today. In Boss Veil's office. He wants my uncle to send money."

"For what?"

Now the whole story came out. She needed to hear what he'd say. She needed to make it all make sense. "For me. Like a ransom. Otherwise, he said, 'Accidents are easy to explain in the woods.'"

Crying overtook her. She couldn't help it. She shivered and let her nose run until she had to blow it on the hem of her skirt, still blue from the envelope. "Do you think my uncle will pay it?" That was the answer she needed, she realized. Why she'd told him the story. She needed him to say she would be all right.

But Red didn't reassure her. In fact, he seemed as if he might not have noticed her crying at all. He sucked in on his cigarette and exhaled through his nose. "I'm not sure. Like I said, I barely met your uncle. But did you say anything to the boss? That you'd found the letter?"

"No."

"Good. That's very good. You don't want to let him know you know."

Red's voice was intense but calm. He was not Esther, who'd be panicking or blaming Lizzie. Red was accustomed to crises. He'd spent decades in the woods where men could lose ears.

He spat onto the log. He ground out the nub of his cigarette into the spit. "We gotta get you outta here. How brave are you?"

"Not very."

"Well, you will be tomorrow."

CHAPTER
TEN

"The block pulley isn't big enough, and we need a new smaller one, too," said Boss Veil with a frown. At the breakfast table, he was marking equipment in a catalog. Men were going into town that morning. Boss Veil held a fat red pencil in his clean, hairless hand. He passed the catalog to Wilton, who squinted at it with his algae-colored eyes.

"The round pulley will be better," he said, passing the catalog back.

"Highway robbery." Boss Veil harrumphed and circled the picture of the pulley.

Robbery, thought Lizzie. You are the thief! And you haven't just stolen my money—you've stolen me. But she said nothing. After last night's confession to Red, she'd had trouble falling asleep, wondering what he'd meant by being brave, but once she'd drifted off she'd slept deeply the whole night through. She was still trapped, but something had been set in motion.

As she watched Boss Veil's pencil run through the logging supplies, checking and circling various things, she had trouble comprehending that he was holding her captive. His fingernails were smooth and trimmed.

His skin was pale and uncalloused. He'd offered her breakfast politely. Pretend you don't know anything. That's what Red had said. Boss Veil was also pretending.

Sun glittered on the water. There was barely a cloud in the sky. The top half of the kitchen door—an old-fashioned Dutch door—was held open with a hook, but there was little breeze to cool the house, only the odor of dirt and fish and rocks. This was the hottest morning so far.

"Very well," said Boss Veil. "I think that's as much equipment as the boat will hold." He dog-eared the page, closed the catalog, and scooted it aside.

He dabbed his mouth with his napkin and clattered his silverware onto his plate. "Fine breakfast," he told Wilton, which meant: clear my plate.

Wilton obliged but stopped halfway. He bent his long body toward the window. His eyes squinted at the horizon. "Is that a tug?"

"A tug?" Boss Veil fumbled at the window seat, found his binoculars, and drew them to his eyes. He adjusted the knobs and scrunched his nose, as if sniffing something unsavory. "It's from Juliana Strait. A huge boom. How did that happen? Why are they selling their wood and we aren't?"

"We *are* selling our wood, boss," reassured Wilton. "But they are too. That's good. That means the mills are buying."

"But not our wood." Boss Veil dropped the binoculars to his lap and pouted like a child.

Lizzie cleared her dishes and set them beside the sink. She wanted to go upstairs and read a chapter before she began her knitting. But before she could excuse herself, there was a knock at the front door.

"Yoo-hoo! Anybody home?" It was Gladys.

She came into the kitchen. Her apron was tied around her slender waist, her dress sleeves were rolled to her elbows, and her forearms were spattered with flour, as if she were still standing in the cookhouse. "I need the girl. I need someone with small shoulders to clean behind the stove."

Boss Veil looked to Lizzie with a question in his eyes. He was not asking her what she wanted, but himself— what he wanted to do with her. "Yes, you can borrow her. But do send her back. Gotta get those socks done. Right, Miss Parker?"

"Yes, sir."

She followed Gladys to the cookhouse. There, in the kitchen, by a large shelf of pans, Gladys handed her a small stack of clothes. They were logger's clothes. A heavy jacket and pants. A layer of wax covered the fabric, as if candles had been smeared on it, and every inch was covered.

Before Lizzie could ask what was going on, Gladys said, "I don't know anything about any of this. All I know is that Red said to put these on, and he'll be here in a few minutes."

"What about the stove?"

"Heavens, girl, that was a lie. Get dressed. And here are the boots." Gladys kicked the toe of a pair of boots on the floor. They were small and worn and had red laces.

"Are those . . . from the wall?"

"Won't hurt you none. Now, hurry."

With that, Gladys disappeared behind a wall of pots and pans. Lizzie felt stiff, almost nauseated. She could not put on the clothes. What were they? A disguise? It was a mistake to have told Red anything. If Boss Veil came into the kitchen and saw her . . .

"I can't," Lizzie called to Gladys, who was clattering at the sink. "I should go back to Boss Veil's house."

"I don't think you should, girl. I don't know what's going on, but if I had to trust either the boss or Red, I'd trust Red."

Gladys was right. Red was trying to help her. Lizzie began unfolding the clothes. There was a jacket with buttons the size of silver dollars and cropped pants. She checked for a shirt, belt, or suspenders, but there weren't any. She looked at her legs in their silly stockings, her seersucker skirt with the pink sash, and her pink blouse.

"Lizzie? If you're going to chicken out, just get outta here," Gladys said.

Get outta here. That's what Red had said the night before. Lizzie thought of the boat that was leaving for town to pick up equipment. Did Red want to smuggle her out of camp?

Lizzie stopped unfolding the jacket. She didn't want to take part in this plan. She should just stay and wait for her uncle to pay the ransom. She could knit socks and play dumb. She looked again at the boots, empty and crumpled, as if waiting for a body that had vanished. A body *had* vanished. Or, been taken to the hospital. She thought of the ear, the hole in the side of a head, the boat filling with blood. *Accidents are easy to explain in the woods.*

She had to leave the island. With quivering fingers, she buttoned the jacket over her blouse. It was nearly the right width in the shoulders but billowed out everywhere else. It was made for a man with muscular arms and a thick middle. The jacket's seams scratched through her blouse. The kitchen was warm from the breakfast cooking, and Lizzie began to sweat, the warmth releasing the stink of the jacket's last wearer.

The pants were heavy and full of grit. The waist was so large—she could've nearly fit another of her inside them—that if she let go, the pants would drop to her ankles. She looked at the sash on her skirt. It was attached to the skirt not by belt loops but tacks of thread. Oh, well, who cares? She yanked off the sash and wove it through the pants as the most ridiculous belt in the world. The pants were so big and thick, the sash nearly didn't tie, but she'd knotted it just as she heard Red's voice.

"Decent?"

"Depends on what you mean."

She stepped from behind the rack of pots. Gladys and Red gave her the once-over, not quite but almost laughing.

"I'll leave you to it," said Gladys and left.

"What's going on?" Lizzie asked.

"Put on the boots," Red instructed. He peered behind him at the porch, then over her shoulder through the windows, toward Boss Veil's house. "Hurry."

Lizzie sat on a bench to lace the boots. Although small for a man, they were too big for her. She could feel where the cleats, the same kind of nails on all the men's boots, had been tacked through the sole. Quickly she laced the boots, which were nearly up to her knee, and wrapped the extra-long laces multiple times around the top as she'd seen the men do.

"You need a hat, too." Red thrust a thick woolen cap into her hands, the cap he'd been wearing on the night she'd arrived. "Tuck in your braids."

"Where am I going?"

"You'll go with the men into Vancouver. But instead of picking up supplies, you'll go to the train station." He handed her a five-dollar bill and pointed for her to put it in her pocket.

"But what if Boss Veil sees me?"

"Gladys is going to delay him at the house. And if you're dressed like that, then he won't see you with those binoculars of his."

"What about my things?" As she asked this, she knew the answer. There was nothing of value in her suitcase. Her money was gone. Her photo was gone. Only her yellow yarn and *Little Women* were left. She felt a tug at her heart but knew she needed to go to the dock, right that moment.

"I told the boys not to ask you any questions. And keep your head turned to the water. Don't look behind you, in case the boss has his binoculars."

She nodded even though her chest was thrumming. She could not breathe deeply enough. Boss Veil had been furious when she'd won at poker. If he caught her trying to escape . . .

"But, what if—"

"There's no time for that," said Red. "And let's not waste time on good-byes either. You have to hurry."

She walked quickly through the woods, careful not to look behind her, her ears pricked for any sound. Once she made it out of the woods, she could see a half dozen men on the dock. They were loading motors, pulleys, hooks, and other unidentifiable equipment into the same motor boat she'd taken on the night of her arrival. The sun beat down. The men's shirts were unbuttoned to the navel.

The tide was low, as low as she'd ever seen it. The whole beach was exposed. Plateaus of moss were drying out. The water near the beach was a yellowish, mossy soup. Froth dried in the crevices of kelp bulbs like spittle on an old man's lips.

Low tide meant that the dock was floating low, so the ramp down to the dock was steep, more like a ladder than a ramp. Closer to ninety degrees than forty-five. She froze at the end of the path and could not proceed to the dock. The ramp was simply too steep. And there were no handrails. It was designed for a man to push a wheelbarrow; she'd seen men doing this, as Olavfur had on the night of her arrival. In fact, she saw now, the narrow strips of wood nailed in place every foot or so were actually two pieces, so that there was a gap in the center for—she figured—a wheel.

But she wasn't a wheelbarrow, or a logger, or an acrobat. She was a girl. She could not climb down. She looked at the water under the ramp. Or, what little water there was. The water was only a few feet deep. She could see nearly every barnacle, rock, patch of seaweed. If she fell, she would break her legs. Or her skull.

Sweat was building up on her forehead, and her skin itched under the woolen cap. Moisture trickled from her crotch to the crooks of her knees. Her boots were humid, her stockings slippery. Yet her hands were cold.

"Come on," said a voice.

On the dock at the bottom of the ramp, a man was gesturing to her. She didn't recognize him. He was older, but not as old as Red. His head was bald at the top, and what hair remained was steel-colored. He wore leather gloves that came up to his elbows. Round spectacles flashed in the sun. He beckoned her forward again, and she saw sweat staining nearly a ring from his shoulder to under his arm.

"You can sit," said the man, "and use the rungs like little steps. You won't fall."

His face was calm. He stood back up and rested his gloved hands on his hips, as if they had all the time in the world, even though Lizzie knew they didn't. What if

Boss Veil was watching, right now, and wondering why a logger was hesitating over the simple ramp?

Elizabeth Parker, you have to do this.

She sat down atop the ramp, like a child at the top of a slide. The ramp was wide enough that, if she looked straight ahead, she could not see the water and rocks below, just the bespectacled man. She extended her legs in front of her. Her boots—she was glad now for them. She bent up her knees and angled her heels toward the plank so that the spikes dug into the wood. The wood was hard and dry, so it was difficult to get real purchase. But she banged hard, and she drove the cleats in just enough to feel secure. She pressed her palms on the rungs by her hips so her elbows were pointed out behind her like a grasshopper's. With a fast suck of air, she scooted her bottom onto the ramp.

The hinges creaked. The wood bounced. One of her boots began to skitter off the rung.

"Ahh!" she cried. The sound didn't ring out over the water but landed limp and pitiful in the heat. She hated the sound. She hated that girl who made that sound. That girl was weak and childish and scared. Lizzie didn't want to be that girl.

The plank was wide. She had legs. She had arms. If she grabbed hold and moved slowly, she would not fall. And she had very thick pants on. The waxy coating was sticky and helped grip the wood. Lizzie slid down another rung. The plank squeaked and bounced again. She made a rhythm with each slide: squeak, bounce, squeak, bounce. And soon enough, she was on the dock.

The man with the spectacles held out his hand and helped Lizzie stand up. He pushed his spectacles up his sweaty nose with one gloved index finger, then cocked his head over one shoulder. "Seat in the boat's ready for you."

CHAPTER ELEVEN

She walked toward the boat and trained her eyes on the oversized nailheads that ran like a spine along the center of the dock. There must be a beam below. In the sun, the parched wood was nearly white.

As Red had promised, the men said nothing. She was relieved. She wanted to feel invisible. To *be* invisible. She thought of Boss Veil's binoculars. *Don't look back. Look ahead.*

The boat, the same one she'd traveled in on the night of her arrival, was so heavy with equipment that only a few feet of the sides rose above the waterline. She worried that adding her weight might send the whole thing to the bottom of the bay. But she had to. None of the men, bustling around the dock, securing knots and tidying things up, offered her a hand, but now that she knew how to keep her knees loose and to step into the middle of the boat, she was able to board the boat without losing her balance.

There was no crate for a seat, and she didn't want to sit on any of the equipment in case she damaged it, so she tugged her jacket cuff over her hand and brushed aside old fishhooks and bird droppings to clear a place for herself on the bottom of the boat. She was glad again for the thick, waxy fabric of her pants, even though so much sweat had collected on her legs that she now noticed a path of moisture dribbling down her calf into the top of a boot.

She wanted to ask how much longer until they left, but didn't want to draw attention to herself. And the men seemed nearly ready. She didn't dare look behind her, but she heard them call out, "Did you load that?" and "Yes," and "Hurry up," and "Let's go."

Four men joined her in the boat. Two sat on the floor with her, and two perched on box-shaped pulleys.

"What are you doing?" one of the men asked toward the dock.

Lizzie looked. A man stood at the edge of the dock, at a small chest-level table, like a podium, as if delivering a lecture. His floppy leather hat was tucked into the waistband at the small of his back. His head was bent down, and his shoulders were working in a busy back-and-forth motion. Over the edge of the podium, he tossed—what was it? A fish tail? Then the head, gills, and balls of pink gut. From the other side, he drew another fish from a bucket and started sawing into it.

"Are those for your girlfriend?" asked the man on the pulley.

"Screw off," said the fish-cutter, not looking over his shoulder.

"Wrong time of day for fish," said one of the men in the hull, to Lizzie. "Those are going to rot in a minute."

The hull smelled of rotting fish, in fact. And gasoline and rust and tobacco. Sweat dripped from Lizzie's forehead into her eyes. She felt lightheaded. She wanted to close her eyes and lie down, but she forced herself to stay upright.

"I'm gonna take these up to the kitchen. I'll be right back," said the man at the podium.

The kitchen! Was he joking? She wanted to stop the man with the fish, to insist that they had to leave right now, but she heard the ramp squeak as he clambered up.

She stared at the toes of her boots. Hurry, hurry, hurry. Let this be over. Let the man return, and let the boat glide into the harbor. Soon all this would be a bad dream. She'd show up at King Street Station in Seattle, dressed in a dead man's clothes, with a story to tell.

The ramp squeaked again. Lizzie didn't dare look behind her, but knew the fish-cutter must be back. Now they could go.

Except the man with the spectacles didn't resume un-cleating the line. He left the knot half-undone, stood up, and put his boot on the cleat. "What can I help you with, boss?"

Boss. Please no. Please, please, please. She didn't meet eyes with the other men in the boat. She just lowered her head even more. Just let him not see her. Please.

"I noticed there was a little delay," said Boss Veil. "What's the holdup?" His voice sounded relaxed, almost friendly.

"We're waiting on Sam," said the man in the spectacles. "He's giving Gladys some fish."

"Fish in the morning?"

The spectacled man sighed and shook his head. Boss Veil chuckled.

Then, more footsteps on the gangplank. The fish errand was over. Sam could get into the boat and they could go. *Hurry, Sam. Please.*

But before Sam could climb into the boat, Boss Veil asked, "Who's that in a rain suit on such a nice day?"

Lizzie almost didn't put it together. One of the men in the boat had to tap her boot. *She* was wearing a rain suit. That's what all this wax was. She couldn't say anything. She couldn't move. Her throat felt swollen shut.

"I'm talking to you, kid," said Boss Veil.

Kid. He knew it was her. She had to look up. She tilted her face slowly, almost squinting, recoiling, as if he were the one who would surprise her rather than the other way around.

"Mm-hmm," nodded Boss Veil, with a smug upturn of his lips. He looked her in the eye with a steely, knowing assessment. "And can you tell me, Miss Parker, where you are headed?"

There was nothing to say. She was cornered. She could give up. Admit it. Ask for mercy.

But she did none of those things. Instead, she held Boss Veil's gaze, looked at the moisture beading on his pink forehead, a softness around his mouth. There was a genuine question in his eye. A sliver of possibility and a moment to think.

"To town," she said. It was the only reasonable answer. And it was, in fact, the truth.

"Why?" asked the boss.

"Umm," she stammered. What would someone do in town? She thought of meeting Red and Freddie that first day. Freddie had been playing poker. "Poker," said Lizzie. "I want to play at one of the card houses in town. I'm sorry. I should've told you."

The boss narrowed his eyes even more. "Why would you play poker in a rain suit?"

She had to say something, now that she'd begun. "It's a disguise, so that they'd let me in the door."

Boss Veil cocked his head. His mouth grew softer. Maybe he was buying the story. "But you don't have any money."

That was true. She had won the poker money, but he had stolen it. But he wasn't supposed to know that she didn't have the money. Her mind was breaking into too many directions, too many lies of his and hers, but she had to answer the question, quickly.

"Freddie gave me some. It was his idea. I was going to play and split the money with him."

Now Boss Veil looked truly surprised. She'd hit upon the right story. It made sense, or at least enough sense, and they both knew it. Boss Veil looked at the men. "Did any of you know about this? Pete, did you?" He glared at the man in the spectacles.

The man—Pete—looked as unruffled as he'd been at the base of the ramp. "I just assumed you knew she was going." His voice was light and simple. For all Lizzie knew, it was the truth. The other men, including the fish cutter, nodded in agreement.

Boss Veil pressed his lips together. His face was growing even pinker. Now he was the one looking cornered, admitting that he'd been tricked by a little girl, in front of his men. He said, "Well, she can't go. I won't allow it."

"I'm sorry, boss," Lizzie said. She stood up, and Pete helped her step onto the dock. "I'm glad in fact not to be going. I know that sounds silly, but I was getting a little scared." She hoped he believed her.

"That's right," agreed Boss Veil. "And you men should've stopped her too. You know better than to send a little girl into town alone. If this happens again, you'll be sorry."

The men nodded. "Should we head out now?" asked Pete. "We should return all this on time."

Boss Veil snorted in annoyance, as if he didn't need to be reminded of the operations of his own camp. "Of course. Go ahead. And Lizzie, you come with me."

Lizzie offered a quick glance of thanks to Pete, and then followed Boss Veil down the dock and up the gangplank. It was easier to climb up now that she knew how to knock her cleats into the wood and press her weight on the rungs. In fact, it was Boss Veil whose fancy shoes slipped on the rungs. But they both made it all the way up, and they were walking through the woods when Boss Veil asked, "Why wouldn't you just leave, if you had money? Don't you want to go home?"

Boss Veil was walking ahead of her, and she was glad he couldn't see her panic. Of course. Her story didn't make any sense at all. But you have to say something, she told herself. Think. She glanced up from the path. The house. Her loft. That was it.

"My things are still here. And Freddie didn't give me enough for a train ticket."

Boss Veil was silent as they climbed the porch. He held the door open for her. Finally, he said, "Very well. Just do not, under any circumstances, try to leave this place again. It was a foolish thing you did. You could've been hurt, a little girl like you on your own. You've gotten too used to being an orphan. But now I'm the one looking after you. Do you understand?"

"Yes. I do."

"Good. Now go knit, as you should've been doing all morning. And get out of that idiotic costume. You're sweating like a hog."

She managed to make it to the loft before the tears came. She stood in the center of the room with her hands cupped over her face. She was trembling too hard to undress. She was humiliated. Exposed. Pathetic. She'd failed, again, in front of everyone. What would she tell Red? Freddie? She'd told a lie about him. Maybe Freddie would tell Boss Veil the truth. Oh, it was all a mess.

Downstairs, Boss Veil uncorked a bottle. She heard a glass clinking, heard him snort after he'd drained his drink. She hated how well the sound carried. Even in her own room, she wasn't alone. She pulled off her hat and wiped her brow, but she didn't undress. Maybe Boss Veil was thinking about how her story didn't add up and he was about to walk upstairs and yell at her. And already her lie was slipping away. Disguise, money, Freddie . . . she would mix it up if she had to answer more questions.

But then the front door opened.

"Are you all right?" It was Wilton's voice.

"Shh," Boss Veil hissed.

The men's voices grew quiet, but she could sense that Boss Veil was telling Wilton what had happened. Lizzie pressed her ear against the floorboards.

"Do you think she knows?" Boss Veil asked.

"How could she?" Wilton was, as always, calm.

"Maybe she guessed, or snooped around, or—I don't know, figured it out."

"You're being paranoid," Wilton said. "She's just a girl who thinks she can play poker and has a crush on Freddie. That's all it is. A silly crush. But she won't be able to escape again. We can order that the men, under no circumstances, are to let her in a boat. And then what could she do? Swim?"

There was a pause. Boss Veil must be seeing the logic. There was no place for her to run. "Fine," said Boss Veil. "But we'll just have to watch her."

With that, Boss Veil said he wanted to check on something at the cookhouse. The screen door banged hard behind him. Lizzie wondered if Wilton would walk upstairs to hear her side of the story, but instead she heard him begin to load kindling into the stove.

Tears began gathering again, but she told herself to stop. She was tired of crying. She was tired of everything. She just wanted to lie down. And get out of her costume. She unbuttoned the jacket, and underneath, as expected, her blouse was soaked through nearly everywhere with sweat. She stepped out of the pants, and her underpants were damp with sweat. She wriggled out of them, wadded them with her stockings, which were stained brown from the boots, and threw them across the room.

Her blouse was too sweaty to mop her forehead well, but she did her best and blotted behind her neck and under her arms. Perhaps later Wilton would provide more water and towels. For now, she tugged her last clean blouse over her head. She paired it with her last clean skirt and second-to-last pair of clean underwear. She sat on the bed and looked at herself. Her bare, girlish legs. The pink striped linen, as fragile as parchment compared to the rain pants. Now her regular clothes were the disguise. She was playing a little girl who would make no more trouble.

How long would she have to play this character? Two weeks: that was how long the mail took, or that's what Boss Veil had said. And her uncle would pay. He was rich. He would pay.

She was too jittery to count stitches, so she opened *Little Women* to an illustration plate. The girls were at a dance. Their hair was curled, their shoulders capped in velvet and lace. Jo was not a real adventurer, just because she lost her temper. Jo had parents—and a home.

Lizzie fingered the smooth illustration and thought of Mary. She imagined telling her about the waxy clothes, the ramp, the man cutting fish . . . She nearly laughed out loud, but she made herself stay quiet because Wilton was downstairs. She had survived another day. Or, morning. She could manage another afternoon, and she wouldn't think further ahead than that. She began a chapter about the dance and Jo's burning her sister's hair.

For supper, she ate sandwiches with Wilton. Boss Veil was in the cookhouse supervising kitchen operations to see if there were ways to cut costs. Wilton didn't mention her rain-costume poker scheme, and neither did she. She managed to eat half of her smoked oyster sandwich.

After she'd cleared her plate, she announced that she needed to use the privy, which was true. Wilton scowled at her. She could guess what he was thinking. He didn't want to walk after her with his bad foot, but Boss Veil would be angry if she went alone.

"I'll be fast," she said. "I'll run."

She gave him a serious look to tell him that she understood. And she did. She didn't want to get in trouble either.

Her first thought when she saw Freddie crouched by the side of the privy was that she didn't have time for him. Just as he said "Lizzie!" she said, "I can't talk to you."

"You have to," he said. "Red told me to check on you."

"So you've been waiting out here?"

Freddie made a gagging face. "I couldn't think of a better place, and I wanted to steer clear of Boss Veil."

"That's for sure."

"So, are you all right?"

"I don't know. I'm alive. Are you in trouble? I'm sorry. I didn't mean to include you in a lie. Did Boss Veil talk to you?" Suddenly she felt terribly guilty. She'd told the lie about Freddie in such a rush, she'd forgotten about it, or it had seemed true even. But of course Boss Veil would be mad.

Freddie didn't look upset. "I just played along. He was mad, but eventually cooled off once I told him I was sorry and would never do it again. But what's going on? Why were you in a boat pretending I was giving you poker money?"

"So Red didn't tell you anything?"

"Only that I should make sure you're all right. So, are you?"

"Yes. I mean, I think so. I'm alive. And I have new shoes." She extended her foot to show her boots, which she was wearing because her Oxfords had been left behind in the kitchen.

Freddie whistled admiringly. "Should I even ask what the story is?"

"Probably it's better you don't know. But thank you for covering for me."

"Sure thing." He nodded, as if it were not even a question. Lizzie's world was changing. In school she'd been the girl who sided with the teachers against the rowdy boys. But now she was grateful for the rowdy boy. She was becoming a rowdy boy herself.

"I should go," she said. "Wilton's waiting."

"Well, will you tell me if you need anything?" Freddie's face was earnest and kind. Part of Lizzie wanted him to embrace her and tell her that he'd protect her, but a larger, better part of her knew that there was nothing he could do to help her.

"I will," she said. "Maybe just a game of cards once I'm off probation."

He swatted her arm but let the back of his hand linger a moment extra. "No way. I've learned my lesson. You can outsmart them all, Lizzie Parker."

CHAPTER
TWELVE

"Lizzie! Hurry!" It was the man from yesterday. Pete. He was at the bottom of the ramp, waving her down. She looked at the rocks below.

"*Lizzie!*" The man was angry. He was not Pete. He was her father. He caught her eye, then looked away. He dove off the dock and began swimming across the bay.

"Lizzie! Get down here!"

It was a voice from downstairs—a real voice. It was Boss Veil. Outside there was shouting.

She pulled on the clothes from yesterday and didn't bother to re-braid her hair. Downstairs Boss Veil was standing with Freddie. She had never seen Freddie, or any of the crew, at Boss Veil's house.

"John Douglass died last night," Boss Veil said. His tone was scornful, almost disgusted. "He had too much to drink and slipped and fell, down by the dock."

She pictured a man slipping on the dock. Banging into a boat, or machine part, or anything. Her mind struggled backward into her dream. The dock, Pete, her father swimming. Now Freddie standing here in Boss Veil's house. She tried to catch hold of something, but everything was loose.

Freddie looked to Boss Veil to ask if he could say something. "We want Lizzie—if you don't mind—if she says yes"—Freddie was stammering, nervous—"to try to punk."

"Punk?" repeated Boss Veil.

"So I can help Olavfur and Sam can take John Douglass's place on main line repair."

Lizzie didn't understand any of this. She didn't want to ask. Her mouth felt thick, her face heavy. It wouldn't matter if she said anything anyway. How she spent her day was for the boss to decide. He scowled at Freddie but didn't say anything. She could tell what he was thinking: he didn't want to let her out of his sight, especially with Freddie, but he didn't want to lose a day's work. Finally he said, "Fine. But no more funny business, you two. And Lizzie, you better learn those codes fast. I don't want another dead man on my hands."

Was she going to be responsible for someone's life? With codes? What codes? Lizzie had so many questions, but all she could do was nod.

Boss Veil swept the air with the back of his hand. "Get going, then."

"Do you have any pants?" asked Freddie, glancing at Lizzie's dress.

She and Boss Veil exchanged knowing looks.

"Go ahead," he said.

Upstairs, Lizzie changed into the wax-coated pants and a plain white blouse. She looked at the boots and imagined her feet sloshing around in them for another day. Maybe she could stuff something inside. Her stockings were filthy beyond hope, and so she wrapped one around each foot, like bandages. She walked downstairs carefully so as not to scratch the floor with the nails on the bottoms of the boots. The stockings felt a bit slimy, but they filled the boots just the right amount.

By the time she walked downstairs, Boss Veil was gone. It was just Freddie, who laughed. "You look like the Tin Man. Or Dorothy dressed as the Tin Man." He made pulling gestures to indicate her braids. Lizzie smiled at the thought of Freddie reading a book about ruby slippers and a lion, and then she thought of herself and Freddie on a yellow brick road. And then all of it—that she, in real life, was a hostage—took her over, and she laughed. Bellowed. The first real laughter since she had arrived at Dark Water Bay. The first laughter in what felt like a long, long time. Maybe since her father's death. Or at least it felt that way.

Freddie smiled hesitantly, then laughed again, but with a note of fragility, like he might cry. John Douglass, she remembered. A man had died. She made herself stop laughing.

"Let's go, giggle-pants." Freddie opened the door for her.

It was only after they'd started toward the woods that Lizzie had collected herself enough to ask, "What's punking?"

"Whistling codes between the choker setter and the donkey."

"There's a *donkey*?" She felt the giggles start again.

"No, that's what we call the steam engine. In the olden days, it actually *was* a donkey. It's the thing that pulls the logs to the beach."

Lizzie thought of the sloped clearing she'd seen on her first day at the beach. The hill with the railroad track and high cables. Maybe she was better off in the loft. Maybe she should have said no.

"You'll see," said Freddie. "But we're already late, so hurry."

She was a fast walker, but Freddie was even faster. She picked up the pace and began to pant. They passed the cabins. They passed where the woods had been cleared. Now, suddenly, the trees were thick together. There was green everywhere. Life everywhere. Life clamoring, bursting, pushing to be alive. Birds called. Spiders hung from ferns. Mosquitoes flew in her ears and down her neck. She popped up her collar and clutched it around her throat.

"Come on," said Freddie. "You aren't a tourist."

But she was! The forest contained more life than she'd ever seen. It was a million emeralds. She was trying to see all of it, to save it, to be part of it—even if it didn't want her. Ferns whacked against her ankles, hips, and shoulders as if trying to press her back down onto the beach. Ahead, ferns were so high around Freddie's waist that he appeared to be wading in a pond.

The trees became larger. As wide as automobiles, foyers, her bedroom loft. There was no way of seeing how tall they stretched because their branches wove themselves into a dense canopy above them.

She stopped. There was a small cave in one of the trees. At its opening, the tree bark curled into a gnarled arch about her height. A cool breeze seemed to emerge from the darkness as if it were breathing.

"What's that?" she called ahead to Freddie, her voice short because her breathing was heavy. "Did someone make it?"

"No. It's just something that happens. Red says that at one camp he was at, there was a big fire and a man was caught in the woods with his dog. Dog was so scared he wouldn't run out to the beach. So the fella saved his dog by tying it up in one of those little caves. Fire just burned right past it. Then the logger came back and the dog was fine."

"That poor dog!" She thought of the dog, panting in the dark, wondering where his owner had gone.

She couldn't imagine a fire. The forest was so green and damp. Even the air was damp. Her face was slick with sweat. Dampness was collecting under her blouse. And the trees were just too *big* for fire. *Nothing* could destroy them. It seemed impossible that they could even be cut down.

But they were. Soon she saw for herself.

She and Freddie reached a clearing where a tree lay on the ground. Many of its branches had been cut off and heaped into piles at the sides of the clearing. The trunk had been sawed into segments, but the tree was so enormous that each piece looked as if it could be a tree of its own. On one such piece, a half dozen men were working with cables and saws and hooks, wrapping up the log as if it were an elephant wrestling to escape.

She noticed a man with spectacles. Pete! He waved and smiled. A hint of a joke. Another morning, and here was Lizzie again, in a place she shouldn't be. She smiled, relieved to see him, and gave him a wave.

Freddie was waving too, but to another man. "Wally!" shouted Freddie.

Wally from poker. He strode over. His long mustache drooped around a humorless frown, and his arms, encased in leather gloves, crossed over his barrel chest. He smelled of leather and tobacco spit. "So it's the card shark, is it?"

"She's going to punk," explained Freddie. "I'm going to take John Douglass's place as climber's assistant."

Wally screwed up his eyes, sizing Lizzie up. His expression was neither friendly nor hostile. Pragmatic. He needed a worker.

"She'll be up and running by the end of the day," promised Freddie.

What sounded like a steam train hooted in the distance.

"Sooner the better," said Wally. "This log is one to be reckoned with. Got to get choking."

Freddie led Lizzie to the far side of the workers, to a large, flat tree stump. It was as wide as a dining room table, the bark nearly a foot thick. The rings were too many to count. Freddie hopped up and sat down, cross-legged. Lizzie joined him, happy for her pants.

"Choking?" she asked.

"Choking the logs." Freddie pointed at Wally and the men. They were laboring with a thick metal cable and a kind of clamp to fashion what indeed looked like a harness wrapped around the log. The end of the cable disappeared down a chute-like clearing downhill through the trees.

"Choking is hitching that log to a cable. When they finish, you sound the whistle so the donkey can start pulling."

Again Lizzie remembered the ski slope–type clearing and the railroad tracks. So that was the problem of logging. Cutting down the trees was one challenge; the other was dragging the logs out of the woods.

"Here." From his pocket Freddie handed her a whistle made of smooth, glossy wood. It was small enough to fit perfectly in her hand. The wood was honey-colored, and its mouthpiece was brass. Its smooth, oval shape reminded her of the slug she had seen in the woods. It felt alive.

Being so close to Freddie's hands made her feel alive too, especially as he passed her the whistle. It felt as if he were passing her something special, a gift, and she had the same tingle as when he'd held out his hand on that first day at the truck. "So once the log is ready," said Freddie, "you whistle one long blow, because that means *ready*. Then the donkey starts and pulls the log."

Lizzie had to force herself to concentrate. She didn't want to appear foolish in front of Freddie. So her job was to whistle commands. That much she was understanding. "But why can't the men whistle themselves?" she asked.

"The men have to have both hands to handle the log. But for now, we wait. There's lots of waiting between the codes." From his pocket Freddie drew a crumpled sheet of paper titled CODES, and he passed it to her. *Go ahead*, said one. Then one dot. *Slack the main line*. Four dots. *Man hurt*. Six dashes.

"It's like Morse code," said Freddie. "Combinations of short and long blows. You gotta memorize them."

"Now?"

"When else?"

"But I don't know what any of this means." *Haul back. Main line. Tight line.*

"You will," he said. "And it doesn't matter yet. Wally will yell, and you'll just blow."

Freddie helped Lizzie memorize the first half dozen codes. Wally, Pete, and the other men were still preparing the log. Men sawed off branches and wrapped cable. Pairs of men dragged branches to the edge of the clearing. Others wiped their brows and drank water from canteens.

Freddie looked to where Lizzie had folded her hands in her lap. They were still red from the laundry. A few small blisters had popped on her knuckles. "Your hands are still in bad shape," said Freddie.

Still. That meant he'd been keeping track.

"My mom takes in laundry for pay," he continued. "She uses tallow and charcoal on her hands."

Lizzie laughed. She thought of the green tube of flower-scented lotion Esther kept by her kitchen sink. "Really?"

"True," said Freddie, not seeing what was funny. Lizzie felt bad for laughing, especially since she might have liked to have some of his mother's concoction right then.

"How did you get to camp?" she asked. "I mean, besides the boat and the truck."

"Through Red. In Horseshoe Bay, where I'm from, I work at a butcher shop during the year. I deliver meat to customers on a bicycle. One year I wore my tires straight through. I was just clattering around the street on the rims." Freddie put his hands out to pretend he was losing his balance. "But these days, people aren't buying much meat. So when Red came to fix the delivery truck one day, we struck up a conversation about logging, and that was that."

"What about your father?" asked Lizzie. "What does he do?"

"He works at the mines out in Cariboo. He's gone most of the year. My sister takes care of the kids while my mom does the pay laundry. My sister's about your age, and then there are three boys. Five, two, and a baby."

"That's a lot of work!"

"That's a lot of *diapers*. Oh! Look! They're almost ready." He pointed to the men. The choker setters were still working on the tree, tightening the cable with the clamp. Wally moved from one side of the log to another, surveying it from both sides, seeming to be looking for symmetry.

"So he's checking to see if the choke is even?" Lizzie asked.

"Very good!" Freddie sounded genuinely impressed. "He doesn't want that log to move at a wrong angle because once it's moving, it's dangerous. Speaking of, that's one of the punk's biggest jobs. Count the men."

"Count them?"

"Before you whistle a command, make sure you have eyes on all the men. That's six of 'em. Because if one's behind the log and it gets rolling toward them, well, then that's a problem. The log can crush a leg in just one second."

She grimaced. "I understand. Count the men before you blow."

"All six."

Then they heard Wally yelling. *"Go ahead!"*

Lizzie could see that the choke was set. Freddie tapped his index finger in the air and counted aloud all six men.

"GO AHEAD!" repeated Wally impatiently.

Freddie handed Lizzie the whistle.

"Me?"

"Yes, you."

"One short?"

He nodded.

She lifted the whistle to her lips. The metal mouthpiece felt cool and delicate, as if a coin. She was too afraid to blow. The knowledge that she would cause the log, something so enormous, to hurtle down the hill overwhelmed her.

"Blow!" said Freddie. "Just calm down and pay attention."

She took a deep breath. She thought of the code: one short. She blew so hard that she felt pins and needles in her cheeks. Sound reverberated through the trees. All that noise from a small whistle. From her.

"Well done!" approved Freddie.

Then came a toot and chug of what must have been the donkey, out of sight down the hill. Then the cable started dragging the log downhill, first slowly and then quickly. The log scraped over rocks and crushed undergrowth. The choker setters stood back and watched carefully. *She* had made that happen. At least a little bit.

"Slack skidding line!" yelled Wally suddenly. Lizzie could see the log was sliding too far forward, so that it was going to jam into the side of the chute and not make it down the hill. The log needed to change direction, fast. She had memorized the code to slack the skidding line:

two short, four short. She blew the code. The donkey hooted again, and after a few moments the log began to roll backward into the center of the chute.

Freddie put his hand out and rested it lightly on her shoulder, to tell her that she ought not to move. "Where are the men? I only see five."

Count the men. Lizzie hadn't counted the men before she blew. She looked frantically at the log. It was still rolling backward, rolling over bushes and rocks and branches—and maybe a man's body.

She counted the men. Only five. She didn't see Pete. She remembered her dream. Pete had turned into her father and disappeared into the water. Now he had really disappeared, under a log. And it was all her fault.

"Please," she said. "Be all right. Please."

Finally the log stopped moving. All of the men stood still, waiting. The donkey stopped its whistling. A crow cawed. Wind shivered through the trees. And then Pete appeared from behind the log. Stumbling but upright. He brushed debris from his pants. The men began shouting, but the world felt silent to Lizzie.

She exhaled but couldn't get a good new breath in. She wanted to vomit. "I didn't count the men," she told Freddie.

"I know." He didn't look to her but to Wally. Wally gave them a serious, warning look. It meant that he was watching her. That this wasn't a game. "Let's get her straight," Wally yelled to the men. Using poles as levers, they rolled the log so that it was aligned with the chute.

Pete was working alongside the other men as if nothing had happened.

"You should do the next code," said Lizzie, thrusting the whistle toward Freddie.

"No. You need to learn. And I'll help you more this time. I should've been paying more attention too."

Soon Wally yelled, "Go ahead easy."

"That's three short?" she asked.

"Yes," Freddie nodded. "But—"

"Count the men." She quieted all the other noise in her mind. She didn't think about Freddie, or Wally, or the log, or anything. Just the men. One, two, three, four, five, six. Then: three short blows.

From far off, the donkey hooted, and then the log was pulled, slowly this time, down through the chute at just the right angle. All six of the men stood watching it.

"Well done," said Freddie, breathing a sigh. "That's all there is to it."

She couldn't tell if he was kidding. But she laughed. A nervous, embarrassed, proud, exhausted laugh.

Freddie laughed too. Maybe he hadn't known that he had said something funny, but now he did. He needed to laugh too. All of the men were safe. Earlier that morning they had laughed because they were nervous, and now they laughed because they were relieved.

They were friends. They understood how to laugh.

After dinner, Boss Veil told her that he wanted her to work as the whistle punk every day. "I'll pay you two dollars a week," he said. He sat in his armchair. His shoes were off, and he wiggled his feet by the fire. Instead of thick wool socks, he wore thin black ones to go with his shiny black shoes.

"Aren't you happy about that?" he asked.

"Yes. I am. Thank you."

She was tired of thanking Boss Veil when she felt the opposite. He would never pay her.

"But Wally told me what happened out there with Pete," said the boss. "He was a medic in the war and is the only man around who can do proper stitches. So don't go killing him."

Lizzie flared hot with shame. Wally had told the boss that Pete had nearly died. Wally must've said how reckless and stupid she'd been, not to count the men. And she had been. It was a terrible mistake. She was about to apologize to the boss, to reassure him that she wouldn't make any more mistakes, but then something stopped her. It was rage. How dare Boss Veil reprimand her. *Accidents are easy to explain in the woods?* No. Accidents are easy to *happen* in the woods. Boss Veil stayed on the beach, or in his office, or in the cookhouse, or away from camp. He was a liar *and* a coward.

Boss Veil turned back to the fire. It popped, and he made a satisfied hum, as if he had put something on to roast. She said nothing, not even good night.

Upstairs, Wilton had set out a fresh washcloth and bowl of water. She rinsed her face and tasted salt from her sweat. She used the cloth to wipe under her arms and down her legs. To find her nightgown, she rummaged past the yellow yarn for the soakers, the ones she'd imagined presenting to Esther at the same time as the hundred dollars. Ha. There wasn't going to be any money at all now, let alone a hundred dollars. Lizzie was headed to Portland for certain.

If indeed she ever managed to leave Dark Water Bay. What if her uncle didn't send the ransom? No. He would. She was his niece, even though they'd never met. She just had to wait two weeks. But even as she told herself this, she wasn't sure she believed it. Her body felt light inside her nightgown, as if she were a ghost.

She heard Wilton come inside the house. The men said good night, and Wilton began to put out the fire. She heard his poker push the logs. Wood broke and embers crackled.

In her anger at Boss Veil, she'd forgotten to use the privy. Now she was in her nightgown. She didn't want to pass Wilton or see Boss Veil. She remembered what Freddie had said when she was afraid to blow the whistle. Calm down and pay attention. She looked around the loft. Lantern, quilt, suitcase. Bench, towel, ceramic basin. That was it. The basin.

But then what? She looked at the little window. It only opened an inch.

She kept her eyes searching her little room. That afternoon Freddie had given her a canteen, and it sat now by the basin. She could pour the contents of the basin into the canteen and then empty the canteen, secretly, in the morning. Then wash it with the shampoo that Wilton had given her. It wasn't so disgusting, if she used soap. No one would find out, would they? Even if they did, so what? She was being held captive in a logging camp where she whistled commands and protected the lives of grown men. So why the heck not pour urine into a canteen.

When she was home, she would tell Mary. They would laugh and be proud.

CHAPTER THIRTEEN

Pay attention.

Two weeks passed, and that's what she did.

She watched the choker setters. She put their images deep in her mind so she could count them without re-seeing. They all wore the same cropped pants, suspenders, high lace-up boots, and long leather gloves, but each had his own variation. Wally had his mustache. Pete had the glasses. A red-haired Scotsman wore a beige knitted vest, and his friend wore a dark, nearly black shirt. The Swedes wore hats: one wide-brimmed and floppy, the other with a stiff brim like a baseball player's.

Between codes, the choker setters sawed off the logs' branches so the logs would slide smoothly through the chute, which she now knew was also called the skid road. The men used metal clamps to secure cables. Before Wally would yell to Lizzie for the codes, he would do final checks of the logs' alignments in the chute. She became so accustomed to his checks that she would have the whistle poised to her lips.

She watched the men fell the trees. The men used axes with metal *T*s at the end of the handles, making two cutting blades. *Double-bit,* the men called this kind of ax, and it did indeed seem as if the ax bit into the tree, creating the kind of bite one could make into an apple. The loggers called the bite a *notch.* Once it spanned a third of the way across the tree trunk, the men would put wood planks called springboard onto either side of the tree, several feet above the ground. A man would stand on each end of the board, and the two of them would pull back and forth on both ends of a saw that was as long as the tree was wide, which was very long indeed.

"Like a two-cylinder engine," said Wally, swishing his index finger side to side as he watched two men sawing. "Bop-bop, bop-bop. That's the secret, getting into a rhythm."

When the tree fell, there were waves of sounds. After the first creak, low at the stump, air rushed up through the branches, and they lifted like wings. Bushes and branches and other things, Lizzie didn't know what all, cracked as the tree fell. Cracked and clattered and burst. When the tree hit the ground, the earth shook. Then came a quiet: once again, no one had died.

She watched the donkey engine. It was rusty and dirty, old-fashioned and patched up, alive with belches and bursts and hoots and chugs. Flames burned in a boiler that Red stoked with wood. Sparks burst out onto moss and needles, and every time, Lizzie was surprised a fire didn't start in the whole woods.

Above the donkey stood a tree whose branches had all been cut off. It was the tallest tree around, perhaps as high as a five-story building. The men called it the *spar*, after a ship's spar. Radiating from it were a dozen or so metal cables, cables secured tightly to the ground and used with pulleys to drag logs along the forest floor. To Lizzie, the spar looked like the center of a Maypole, if the cables had been ribbons and the logs dancing children.

Many days Olavfur dangled from the spar in a harness. The high climber, they called him. He cleared branches and worked on the lines. He was so high that just watching him made her stomach drop. One day at lunch, he sat with his back against a stump, apart from the group of men but close enough to see that Lizzie wasn't eating her sandwich. It was liver and mustard oil. It smelled like dog food. The oil had seeped onto her apple, and she wiped it off with the napkin.

"Do you want cheese?" asked Olavfur. He held up a hunk of white cheese as big as his fist. "Gladys gives me more food because I am more man." He wasn't trying to be funny. It was the language. He said man like *MAH-n*. Food was *foot*.

"No, thank you. I am not more girl." She gestured to her body. She was half Olavfur's size, or a third. A wisp in comparison. But a hungry wisp, so when he offered again, she accepted the cheese. She tried to eat slowly to make it last, but now that the taste was in her mouth, she gobbled it up more quickly than she'd eaten anything.

From then on, Olavfur brought her lunch. Perhaps he'd asked Gladys for more food. Perhaps he'd explained the situation. Perhaps he was giving her his own food.

No matter how many times she said she didn't need the food—a lie—he gave it to her. Not just cheese. Bacon and jam sandwiches. Roast chicken on plain bread.

Some days Olavfur ate in the tree, in his harness. Freddie brought food to him. They'd meet halfway down the spar. That was Freddie's new job: assisting Olavfur. Freddie sharpened the axes and hatchets and saws. He took the sharp ones up and brought the dull ones down. He took water and food and fresh towels to wipe Olavfur's brow. Freddie worked with great pride and concentration. It would be very far to fall.

"That's for the bad injuries," said Freddie one day at lunch. He pointed to the bottom of the spar, by a shed that held axes and saws. There was an old-fashioned bell that reminded Lizzie of the Liberty Bell.

"What happens if you ring it?" she asked.

"Men at the beach get a boat ready in case someone needs to go to the hospital. The boss comes to the woods."

She lifted one of her boots. "Is that what happened when this fella lost his ear?"

"It's like the whole forest is ringing."

Dark Water Bay was alive. Ravens darted and screeched. Bald eagles nested in high trees. Egrets dragged their beaks across glossy evening water. Garter snakes and wild mink slithered into rocks. Seals watched everyone and everything, their shy helmets appearing and disappearing into the bay.

There was light. At breakfast, flat pearl. By noon, full gold. It shone through the trees as if through a cathedral's windows. Some patches of dirt were nearly black with shadows. Patches in the sun were orange with wood chips and dry tree needles. This light was hot and smelled of ferns and mildew. By evening, the sky was a luminous bruise. By night, a pure black.

Rain came. The bay was an acre of pitted slate.

Everyone wore tin clothes like Lizzie's. The men hung their jackets on nails on the cookhouse walls. The smells at meals were of wet hair, wet wool, and wet dirt. The men ate in underwear shirts. No one complained, not even once, and so neither did Lizzie, even though her boots were lakes of rain.

She finished re-knitting the socks and wore them herself. She washed them in the evenings with hot dishwater, wrung them out, and laid them by Boss Veil's hearth overnight. The wool was so thick, the socks never fully dried out, and they always smelled of smoke. After the rain, when she sat between codes, if she knew she had a while, she'd take off her boots and socks and stretch her toes in the sun. She wondered if she had ever known such pleasure.

Some days there were very few codes. On one of these days, Wally asked her to sew buttons on a shirt, then patch a hole in some pants. Soon other men had other projects. She repaired seams and reattached belt loops. She darned socks, sweaters, and hats. She used the twine-like yarn, and patches of brown spread among the men like mange.

For herself, she cut apart the dress with the ink stain at the hem and sewed it into a blouse and pantaloons for a layer under the rain suit. She liked the pantaloons so much that she converted another skirt too. That way she could wash her clothes on a rotation and let them dry a full day. She clipped them to a tree branch on a knoll overlooking the bay.

She did her washing after dinner and fell into the routine of staying on the knoll to read. She brought a lantern and extra clothes to wrap around her neck and legs against the mosquitoes. When she returned, Boss Veil would ask, "Do you think kerosene is free?" And she would think, *I am working for free.* She began staying out past his bedtime. She knit herself a second pair of socks.

One night when she returned, it was so late that Wilton was setting up his bed.

"Am I keeping you up?" she asked. "I'm sorry. I used to sleep in a parlor and I hated it." As soon as the words were out of her mouth, she regretted them. Wilton was an adult, not a child. For Wilton, this bed was where he always slept. Or was it?

"Do you live here year 'round?" she asked.

Wilton piled cushions from the back of the bench onto the armchair, except he saved one out to shake into a white pillowcase. He spread a white sheet over the cushions on the seat of the bench. Over that, he spread a gray boiled-wool blanket that had black overstitches along the edges. The blanket reminded her of war and the bedrolls she'd seen on the boat coming from Vancouver.

Such a long silence passed that she worried he hadn't heard the question, or had decided not to answer. "Good night, then," she said, embarrassed.

"I don't," said Wilton, spreading out a sheet. "None of us does. The logging shuts down. There's snow, and it gets dark at three o'clock in the afternoon. The men work in the mines or docks, if they can. I worked in the mail office of a leather supplier, or I did last winter. But they've fallen on hard times now. I hope I find something else because I won't fare so well at a hobo camp."

He untied his shoes and tucked them under the bench. He pulled off one sock, then the other. One foot was wooden. It looked like what her father would put into a dress shoe to keep its shape. The ankle was two rods of metal.

"Gladys stays at camp all winter," said Wilton. "She scares away the squatters and otters. They shit all over the dock, and then it dries out and ruins the wood."

"The squatters, or the otters?"

"The otters. Gladys pisses to keep them away. Does it at night because that's when they want to do their business. It's marking territory, and she wins."

Wilton cupped a hand over the knee of the leg with the bad foot. Through his pants, with his thumb and forefinger, he fiddled with something that sounded like a latch, and then pulled the wooden foot and metal shin from his pants. He winced slightly. He closed his eyes and arched his back, and she imagined he was stretching out the real foot that used to be there.

He pushed his leg under his bed. "The other fellas like this"—he gestured to his leg—"they don't have any place to go."

Something clattered on the porch. "For crap's sake!" yelled Boss Veil. He stumbled through the door, catching his weight on the wall. "One day I'm going to trip over that cat and die, and I'm going to blame you." He waved a finger at Wilton.

Boss Veil had been to the privy. He was wearing his white long underwear, no socks, and his unlaced dress shoes. His eyes were half-open, his face red and swollen—as if from crying, but it was the drinking.

"That cat doesn't even catch the rats. We should've thrown her out with the others." Boss Veil was speaking to no one. He stumbled into his room and shut the door.

"Thrown her out?" Lizzie asked Wilton.

"When we got here in May, there was a pack of kittens, left here by some sailors. They keep cats on board to catch vermin, but they don't need the kittens. They ought to drown them, not pass them on to other people, but they don't. So I put the litter in a bag and dropped it out in the bay, but I kept one kitten. And Boss Veil is wrong. She does catch a good rat or two."

Lizzie's dreams were filled only with whistle codes. Short, long, short, long. Long, short, long. By morning, it was a relief to go to the woods and do the work.

CHAPTER FOURTEEN

One day at lunch, Freddie was sliding a long, tapered metal file in between the teeth of a handsaw about three feet long. He propped one end on the dirt and one end on his knee and slid the file back and forth as casually as if he were a woman tending her fingernails. The filings glinted in the sun and drifted onto a trail of ants.

"There's an ax over there that Olavfur wants sharp by the end of lunch, and I still need to finish this saw. Would you mind fetching it for me?"

Lizzie had finished eating. Freddie pointed to a tree stump that looked three times her height. The stump was quite high, enough for springboards, and above one of the boards an ax was angled into the bark.

"Just hop up on the springboard. You'll be tall enough to reach, I think."

Lizzie wasn't worried about reaching the ax. She was worried about climbing onto the board. From her vantage point it appeared more than a yard off the ground, and there was no obvious way to step onto it.

Lizzie thought of saying that she couldn't even climb a school gate. She nearly hadn't made it down the gangplank to the dock. But Freddie hadn't seen that. In fact, he looked at Lizzie as if retrieving the ax were a perfectly reasonable request. "All right," she said.

But as soon as she reached the tree, she regretted agreeing. The plank was high off the ground. Too high. Nearly to her shoulders. She glanced behind her, worried that the men were watching. Was there something she could step on? She scanned the ground for a rock and spotted a round hunk of metal. Some sort of pulley? It didn't matter what—just that it was about two feet tall and could survive being stepped on.

But now what? She still had to maneuver herself onto the plank, and the pulley was starting to sink, lopsided, into the soil. Above her, a stub of a branch was almost within reach, so she stood on her tiptoes. Just as the pulley was tipping over, she grasped the stub as if it were a handle and swung first one leg and then the other onto the plank.

Her heart thumping, she released the branch stub, pushed her palms flat against the tree trunk, and balanced on the plank. It squeaked and sagged under her weight, and she reminded herself that the logger who'd left the ax must have been twice her weight—but luckily not twice her height. With another stand on her tiptoes and a firm pull, she was able to pull the ax from the tree.

Now what? The pulley had tipped over. The soil below the tree was studded with rocks. Jump? Holding the ax? No. She tossed the ax to the ground and then, careful to avoid it, jumped herself. She stumbled and caught her weight on her palms.

"Well done," said Freddie as she handed him the ax. She smiled. She had climbed up a tree and retrieved an ax. She had never done either of those things before, and here she was, having done both.

Her palms were hot and throbbing. She noticed that blood was slowly filling small gash marks. And, in the center of her palm, there was a black lump the size of a pea. Peering more closely, she saw that it was a pebble. She tried to brush it away but saw that it was lodged under the skin.

This had happened once before, when she was running on the sidewalk as a little girl. Her father had scrubbed her hands with dark brown soap and had her soak her hands in a pot of hot water to soften the skin. Then, with a long pair of tweezers, he'd removed the pebble while she'd looked away.

"Is there soap out here?" she asked Freddie. "Or tweezers, or a bandage?" She turned her palms so he could see.

"No. Only some turpentine and clean rags in the toolshed. Want one?"

"No, thanks."

Freddie yelled toward Wally. "Anything going down the chute soon? Lizzie here needs to go down the hill."

She wished he hadn't said anything. She could survive. But just as she was about to protest, Wally said, "She's got an hour."

Lizzie ran down the hill back to the boss' house. She hoped there'd still be warm water from the breakfast dishes. Even without the fire burning, on the surface of the wood stove, in cast-iron pots, water stayed hot nearly all day. Indeed there was water. Even better, the house was empty.

As she ladled water into a shallow bowl, she noticed something. A full bottle of whiskey next to the one with only an inch left. An unopened jar of jam that had a label tied with twine. MINK COVE RASPBERRY.

Mink Cove. Someone had been to pick up the mail. And two weeks had passed since Boss Veil had mailed his ransom note. Enough time for something from her uncle. Lizzie didn't bother soaking her hand. Quickly, she washed her palm with soap and pressed the pebble from its pocket of skin with a butter knife.

The key was in the Folger's can, and she opened the office door easily. She needed to be fast. Wilton was likely in the cookhouse or the commissary, and Boss Veil down at the beach, but she couldn't be sure.

Luckily, the mail was in plain sight. A tidy stack in the center of the desk blotter.

Her pulse raced as she picked up the stack. About a half dozen envelopes, all unopened. She flipped through return addresses from mills and suppliers and a bank. Nothing from her uncle. She looked through the envelopes again, looking for the handwriting she'd seen on the letter at Esther's table. Nothing.

It couldn't be. She didn't understand. She'd thought her uncle would send money. She'd *known* it. He was rich. She was in danger. He must've sent the money. She started to look around on the desk for more mail, but then footsteps sounded on the porch. Fast. Not Wilton's. The front door opened, and then the office door. Lizzie twirled to face Boss Veil. She was still holding the stack of mail.

Boss Veil looked at her, then the mail. "What are you doing?"

There was nothing clever to say. No lie about knife pleats or poker. But she had to say something. "I was just . . . seeing if my uncle had written."

"Your uncle? Why would your *uncle* be writing?"

Oh, no. She should've said sister. She wasn't supposed to know about her uncle.

Boss Veil stepped closer. "I asked you. What do you know about your uncle?"

"Nothing. I just—I—"

"You rat. You've snooped in here before, huh? I told Wilton that. Is that why you tried to escape? You knew about your uncle, and my little plan?"

"I don't know what you're talking about."

"Yes, you do. Let me tell you the whole story, since you're such a curious girl. Your uncle owes me money. He promised to invest in the camp, and then he didn't. And when he left, he left behind a letter for Wilton to mail to say that you shouldn't come to camp. But I didn't send it because I thought you *should* come to camp." He smiled. His eyes twinkled, as if he wanted her to praise his clever scheme.

His smile turned into a sneer. "But it turns out you are a little sneak. And a worthless sneak, it seems. Your uncle doesn't seem to want to pay."

So it was true. Her uncle hadn't sent the money. Her throat swelled shut. The room, barely larger than a pantry, seemed to shrink around them.

Boss Veil stood between her and the door. He squinted at her, then looked past her at the desk. He stepped so close that his belly brushed against her sash. He reached around her to something on the desk. Her back was to the desk, and she couldn't see what it was until it flashed out of the corner of her eye. Scissors.

He kept the blades shut, like a dagger, and pressed the tips under her chin. The metal was heavy and cool. Coolness spread down her neck and through her chest. Her breathing was shallow. Boss Veil dragged the scissor point along her jawline and stopped under her ear. Her pulse throbbed.

She didn't open her mouth wide, feeling the scissors' pressure. "Maybe I can ask my uncle for the money myself. I can ask my sister."

"Your sister!" said Boss Veil. "I almost forgot. Here . . ." He fumbled through the mail behind her, pressing the scissors into her neck even more.

With one hand, he shook out a letter and held it so she could see. It was Esther's writing. He read in a cutesy, mocking voice. "'Dear Lizzie, I'm so pleased to know you've arrived and are doing well. We miss you here, although we are able to charge the boarders even more than we'd thought. Robert enjoys the extra activity in the house.'" Boss Veil stopped and caught Lizzie's eye. "I sent dear Esther a telegram to say you'd arrived safely." He winked. "There's more to the letter, but it's a bit dull. Some details about your brother-in-law's job search. He hasn't found anything yet."

Lizzie could barely stand it. Writing to Esther and now reading her letter seemed more an invasion than stealing her things. But there was nothing to say. She looked at Boss Veil with wide, trembling eyes. *Take pity, please.*

Boss Veil tossed Esther's letter on the desk. Then he tilted his chin up and peered at her neck and ear. He tugged a section of hair out from one of her braids. "This'll do," he said. He nestled his scissors tight against her scalp, yanked the hair so hard she shut her eyes, and snipped.

"Done. You can calm down. Here, don't you think this'll be a nice gift for your uncle? No one else at camp has such nice hair." He held up the hair. Proof she was at the camp, for the ransom.

The boss curled the hair into a circle and set it on the desk. "It's worth one more try," he said. "And if he doesn't send the money, then . . . who's going to ask questions about a poor little orphan?"

Clong! Clong! Clong!

Lizzie and Boss Veil both held still. The bell clonged again. It must be the bell she'd seen up the hill, by the donkey. The one reserved for serious injuries—or worse.

Boss Veil walked ahead of her into the woods. His fancy shoes slipped on the path, and he had trouble keeping his balance. She was accustomed to walking fast with the loggers, and she wanted to kick him to make him hurry up. She was afraid. Who had been injured? Red or Freddie or Olavfur? Or Wally or Pete or another choke setter? Or any logger. She couldn't bear to see any of them hurt.

Finally they made it up the hill. By the base of the spar, Freddie was sitting on a log, doubled over in pain, clutching one shoulder. His face was white and covered in sweat. His eyes were closed. He rocked back and forth and moaned.

"Goddammit," hissed Boss Veil. He marched over to Freddie and crouched to look in his face. "What did you do, boy? Can you hear me? What did you do?"

Freddie didn't open his eyes. He rocked forward and retched onto the ground.

Pete was standing next to him. He pulled a bandanna from his pocket and wiped Freddie's mouth. "He fell," said Pete. "It's a dislocated shoulder." Lizzie remembered what Boss Veil had said about Pete's being a medic in the war.

"Can he still climb?" asked Boss Veil.

"No," said Pete. It was obvious even to Lizzie that Freddie was in no shape to climb. "I have to pop the shoulder back in, and then he'll need to heal."

Boss Veil looked to Olavfur. "Can you get the pulleys down by yourself? They're already past due."

Lizzie remembered the pulleys in the boat on the day of her attempted escape.

"I've already done it, except for one." Olavfur pointed to a small pulley a third of the way up the spar tree. "My arm is too big to reach inside and release the pin. It was a job for Freddie."

"Goddammit, Freddie!" yelled Boss Veil. His face was red. He raked his hands through his hair and then pressed his fingers over his eyelids. Slowly, he removed them. "Can't someone else do it? Red, you are small."

"I'd prefer to die another way," he said.

"I don't care. You and Freddie are the only shrimps we've got. Aside from her"—he gestured to Lizzie— "and she's no help."

No help. Lizzie felt something bristle inside her. She didn't know how to climb a tree, that was true, but it couldn't be true that she was no help at all. She could hike into the woods faster than Boss Veil. She was a good whistle punk. She had survived in camp this long, hadn't she?

"I can do it."

"You?" Boss Veil looked at Lizzie first as if he hadn't heard her, and then with amusement. "Truly?"

"You don't have to," said Pete. He had popped Freddie's shoulder back into place and was now wrapping his arm in a sling made from an old shirt. Freddie's face was wan. He had his eyes open but was staring blankly at the dirt. "We can try to figure out another way. Maybe a tool. I just don't want to see another child hurt today. Or worse."

She shouldn't have said anything. Pete was right. She couldn't climb that enormous tree. She looked to the spar and tried to imagine herself in Olavfur's harness. The pulley the men were pointing to was up as high as a two-story house. Aside from retrieving the ax for Freddie, she had never climbed any part of a tree. "Never mind," she stammered. "You're right."

"You can do it."

It was Olavfur. He stepped forward from the crowd. He towered over the other men. His sleeves were rolled up, and his gloves were tucked under his suspenders. His face was serious. "She is strong. I will help."

Pete looked to Lizzie. She remembered his calmness as he'd waited for her at the bottom of the gangplank. But now his expression was different. He was afraid.

Lizzie was about to say she really couldn't do it, but then Olavfur said, "You can try."

Try. That meant one step. She could turn back if it looked too hard. A feeling took over her. Light and free and fast. She had gone far into the woods, but she was about to go farther.

She followed Olavfur to the spar. He was the tallest, broadest man at the camp. His suspenders formed a Y across the thick muscles in his shoulders. She thought of Freddie's smaller yet also muscled arms and back. She was nowhere—nowhere—near as strong as these climbers.

With every step toward the spar, her pulse quickened. She felt as if bricks were tied to her boots, but she also felt as if her legs might float off her body in the wind. The breeze had picked up. A few of the yarding cables shivered and made ghostly, high-pitched sounds. Of all times to be windy.

From behind, she felt the loggers' stares. She would have preferred it if they had been making hoots and hollers, but instead they were silent, as if she were marching to her death. She felt exposed, as obvious and bare as the spar itself.

She called to Olavfur. "I can't."

He stopped and turned. His expression was kind, yet impatient. "I have a daughter in Sweden. She is strong and brave. Like you." Lizzie could tell that he wanted to say more but didn't have the right words in English. She pictured him cradling a blue-eyed baby girl. He wouldn't risk Lizzie's life. Or at least, that's what she thought. But what if his daughter was a different kind of girl? Stronger?

Olavfur motioned her forward. "Come on," he said, walking again, and she was pulled along by his motion.

They arrived at the base of the spar. There, a long, thick rope was looped three times around the tree. Attached to it was a swath of leather and a metal chain. He began tying and cinching the materials with an easy competence. For him, all this was normal.

She looked up. The spar's height was so great, she felt as if she were tipping backward.

He stopped cinching the ropes and made a large loop of rope on the ground. "Step inside," he said. She did. He wrapped ropes around the tree and her waist, then made a U-shape of chain underneath her thighs and adjusted the wide leather belt snugly around her lower back. A harness. "Sit."

The leather dug into her back, the chain into her thighs, but she felt secure. Her face was less than a foot from the bark, and her knees knocked against it. The trunk was so wide that she couldn't see anything on the other side.

"These are pliers," said Olavfur. He slid a small pair of pliers into a pocket in the leather belt. "You can use them to pull out the pin."

"What's a pin?"

Olavfur held up his index finger and pointed inside a circle he formed with his other hand. "It's in the middle of the pulley, like this. You'll just pull with the pliers, and the pulley will fall."

Lizzie could picture how this would work. She patted the pliers and nodded.

"Now spurs," said Olavfur. She lifted her boots one at a time as he fitted them with metal spikes at the front. She felt like a strange monkey: the ropes were long arms hugging the tree, the spurs knife-like toes.

Then he motioned for her to kick her spur into the bark. "Hard. And pull yourself up with the rope."

He hoisted her back and her thighs—she tried not to be embarrassed—as she kicked into the tree and grabbed the ropes. Then, to her surprise, he let go, sending her thighs hard onto the chains and her hands sliding hot down the prickly rope.

"Ow!" she winced. The pebble in her palm had felt like nothing compared to this.

"Gloves." Olavfur handed her a pair of battered and stained leather gloves. They were so large that they reminded Lizzie of baseball mitts. The openings sloshed around her wrists. Her fingers barely made it halfway up the finger slots. But her bare skin wouldn't survive the ropes.

"Now step again," instructed Olavfur. "Both feet. One after the other. Up."

She punched her spurs higher up the tree and forced herself to stand, half leaning into her harness—but the harness was slipping.

"Lift the rope!" Olavfur said. The rope looped around the other side of the spar. The rope was hard to grasp because her gloves were so loose. It took all her strength to lift the loop of rope another foot up the tree.

"Again," he said. "Step, step, lift."

Step, step, lift. One spur, other spur, lift the rope. She had climbed only a few feet off the ground and already her arms were tired. As tired as they had ever been. They burned; they felt soft. "The rope's too heavy."

She glanced down at Olavfur. After all this effort, her feet barely reached the top of his head.

"You are safe in the harness," he said. "You can rest."

Resting meant sitting on the chain that dug into her thighs. The pain encouraged her to jam her spurs into the tree, lift the rope, and step.

Step, step, lift.

"Good," he encouraged. "Just like that."

Step, step, lift. And she connected the motions to another step, step, lift. Her body was becoming less tight, her movements a little more fluid. At that moment, she was learning something: fear was strongest when she did nothing. Once she started to move, she could conquer it. She kept moving.

CHAPTER
FIFTEEN

She climbed three times the height of Olavfur. Her legs were strong from hiking in and out of the woods. Step, step, lift. Don't look down.

She was breathing hard. Her arms began to tremble. They weren't as strong as her legs. They wouldn't make it the whole distance. No—that wasn't true. No matter how much they burned, they wouldn't snap off her body. She would burn them through, and they would still be all right. She heaved the rope once more.

She could see from the angle of the yarding cable that she was more than halfway to her goal.

In spite of herself, she looked up. Immediately, the tree seemed to sway backward as if it were a mast on a pitching ship. She felt that she was tipping backward. Her stomach rolled. Bile sloshed into her throat. Bark crumbled under her spurs, and before she knew it, her legs were churning in the air as if pedaling a bicycle. She clung to the rope with all her strength and pulled her body toward the tree. Curling her toes inside her boots, she stabbed one spur and then the other into the tree.

Step, step, lift.

Don't look up.

The chain under her thighs felt as if it had sliced to the bone. The gloves stank with sweat. Pitch dripped into her hair. Dirt stung her eyes, and blisters began to bubble on her heels and toes. She made it halfway, two-thirds, three quarters. She heard a cheer from the men below.

It was then that the wind blew. It felt like the ocean, swooping up waves underneath her. Her harness swung back and forth. The rope creaked. The yard lines shrieked. Branches of nearby trees rattled and thrashed and swept. Fir cones fell.

Her harness swung so violently that her legs lost contact with the tree. Her spurs scraped across bark. She couldn't steady the harness no matter how hard she pulled on the ropes. Forget what she had thought earlier: now her arms felt as if they really *were* snapping off her body. She let go with one hand. Olavfur's glove was snatched into the wind and flew out of sight.

Hanging by a single arm, she couldn't help but collapse into her harness. Her knees caught the chain, but her thighs fell through. The leather strap skidded to her shoulders. If the strap slipped above her head, she would flip backward and fall.

Maybe this was supposed to happen. Maybe she was supposed to die. She could just let go, and then everything would be over. The world didn't need her. Esther was far away. Her uncle didn't want her. Her father was gone. She ducked her chin close to her chest and closed her eyes.

But you *aren't gone,* said a voice in her head. *You are here. Try.*

She opened her eyes. The wind slowed. The air grew quiet. Her harness was still. She arched her back to shimmy the leather down from her shoulders. She wriggled her thighs to try to scoot the chain back under her.

She knew she needed to act now, before the wind picked up again. She stabbed one spur into the tree so forcefully that she nearly buried it in the bark, and then the other spur. With her legs secure, she was able to use her free hand to sit back up in the harness. Now she was able to grasp the rope with both hands—and release the hand that had been holding on for so very long. She stretched out her cramped, blazing fingers.

Her every muscle shuddered. She worried that if she let herself rest any longer, her body would shut down entirely—or the wind would start back up. She could tell from the angle of the yarding lines that she was near her goal. She stepped a few inches and tossed the rope barely a foot. Then half a foot, a few inches, barely an inch, until she reached out to a small wooden boom that extended from the spar tree. With the other hand she took out the pliers. She could see the pulley attached to the yarding line. It was about a foot in diameter, and in the middle was what looked like a pin. She reached the pliers through a small opening between two cables and touched the pin attaching the pulley to the longer cable. She reached her arm as far as it would go, and even then she could barely reach the pin. She grasped the pin in the jaws of the pliers. She tried to twist the pin, but it was stiff. She tried again, and it moved a little. She turned it again and pulled it out. The pulley fell. Straight and hard. If someone had been below it, they would've been killed, just like that.

The men cheered, but she barely heard them. She put the pliers back into her belt. She didn't feel victorious. She felt afraid again. She had been marking progress as if her goal were only to go up—and not back down again. After nearly sliding through her harness that one time, she understood how carefully she would have to descend.

She pulled her spurs out of the bark and stepped down. She tugged down on the rope. To her horror, the rope slid down the tree twice as fast and as far as she had anticipated. In order not to have her harness go slack, she ripped her spurs from the tree and let herself free fall for a moment until she could feel the harness tighten. She punched the spurs back into the bark.

Her gloveless knuckles grated down the bark. They stung with splinters, but she willed herself to ignore the pain and to pay attention to strategy. She looked up and gauged how far the rope had descended with the one tug. She calibrated how far she ought to descend on each throw of the rope. She sucked in her breath, balanced on the tips of her spurs, tugged the rope, and forced herself to drop as far as the rope let her.

Tug, drop, stop. The falling sensation terrified her, but she also knew it would get her down soon. A bona fide logger now, she cursed. One terrible word after another.

And then she was down. As soon as her boots touched something solid, her knees buckled and she toppled to the ground. Olavfur unhooked the chains and leather, scooped her up like an infant, and laid her gently onto a spongy bed of moss and fir needles.

"Are you hurt?"

Her arms felt as if they were levitating off the ground. The backs of her thighs were hot and bruised. Every muscle quivered. "I lost your glove," she said.

Olavfur laughed. Then, in a tender voice, he said, "I am sorry. If I had known about the wind, I would have never sent you up. You are a strong, brave girl."

He held up her head so that she could sip water from his canteen. He rinsed her bloody knuckles, the sting of the water almost unnoticeable compared to the sting of the wounds. He unlaced her boots. She winced as sweaty blisters rubbed in her socks. She propped her cramped back against a tree stump. Breeze chilled her sweat-soaked clothes, and she shivered.

The loggers clapped. Red hooked two fingers in his mouth and whistled. Pete had his arms crossed over his chest, still disapproving. Wally shook his head in a way that meant, "Who'd have thought?" Boss Veil was nowhere in sight. He'd probably headed down the hill when it had become clear that she was going to succeed. She hated him for that but was relieved he was gone. For now.

She hobbled through the crowd to find Freddie. He was sitting where he had been, but color was back in his face. "Wow-wee. I can't believe it," he said.

"Me either. Are you okay?"

He scooted over on the log so she could join him. She sat down.

"I think I saw God there for a while," said Freddie. "I gotta say, I'm not too keen on hanging by ropes any time soon. I think you should do it."

"Me? Climb?"

"Well, you didn't get swept away in a windstorm. That's pretty good. I'll teach you how to sharpen the saws, and I'll go back to punking. At least for a little while."

But he'd wanted the climbing job so badly! He must've seen the pity on her face. "Hey," he reassured her. "I've still got my ears."

She didn't laugh. She was working something out in her mind. If she were Olavfur's assistant, and the job needed to be done . . . then she was safe. Boss Veil wouldn't hurt her, even if the ransom money didn't come. Without thinking, she put her hand on Freddie's knee to steady herself. She kept it there, and he didn't push it away.

"You have pitch in your hair," said Gladys as Lizzie was clearing her plate after supper.

Lizzie felt the back of her head. Near the base of her braids was a clump of something sticky. "Follow me," said Gladys. Lizzie hadn't spoken to Gladys since the morning of her escape attempt, and Lizzie's first instinct was to say she didn't need help. But Gladys had tried to help her before, and maybe she could help her now. Lizzie needed to get the pitch out somehow.

As fast as she could, given her throbbing thighs, Lizzie hobbled after Gladys through the kitchen until they stopped next to the food pantry. Through a small door was Gladys's room. Inside sat a bed, dresser, and vanity with a tall mirror. The walls were painted a fresh white, and blue-flowered curtains matched a blue-flowered bedspread. No dust, no stray fir needles. The air was cool and scented with soap.

"Sit," said Gladys, her voice no less gruff despite the surroundings. She gestured to the vanity's blue-upholstered stool. "Undo your braids." Lizzie did so as Gladys unscrewed a familiar bottle marked turpentine. Gladys passed Lizzie a handkerchief, white with embroidered edges, to hold over her nose.

Lizzie straightened her posture so that Gladys wouldn't have to stoop too far, although Gladys was so tall that she'd have to stoop no matter what. Without explanation or apology, she began rubbing the pitch with the turpentine rag.

Over the past three weeks, Lizzie hadn't seen herself except in glances in Boss Veil's small, black-streaked shaving mirror. The sun had given her freckles and tanned cheeks. Against the new coloring, her green eyes shone especially bright. She studied herself hard, the way she always had done in a mirror, to see if she looked pretty. But now she was doing something else. She was trying to see something she couldn't see. Something that would tell her who she had become when she had climbed that tree.

She didn't see any single thing. But she was changed. She was something new. She was moving. She felt as if she were still climbing the tree.

"You're going to light on fire if I keep using more of this stuff," said Gladys. She went across the room, opened her closet, and returned with a box. Inside were sewing supplies, including a heavy pair of silver fabric shears. She held the shears in one hand as she lifted Lizzie's hair off her neck and tucked it under to make it look like a bob. If she noticed the place where Boss Veil had cut, she didn't say.

"I think it's time for a new 'do," said Gladys.

"Can't you just cut off the piece with the pitch?" asked Lizzie.

"People will think you've been in the loony bin. Plus, isn't this the style for girls your age?"

La-di-da, Esther would say. Aren't you just Miss Fashion Plate?

Lizzie looked at herself. She liked the way the hair hit beneath her chin and made her face look sharper. And short hair would be so much easier to wash with that basin on the porch. "Go ahead," she said.

Gladys draped a towel around Lizzie's shoulders. Without preamble, she sliced off a hunk of hair below Lizzie's right ear. By the time Gladys was finished, there were no stray pieces or odd angles. Lizzie might have expected such a cut from a real beauty parlor.

"All done," said Gladys, shaking the hair off the towel and onto the floor. Lizzie rubbed the nape of her neck. Skin and air. The hair was just . . . gone.

Gladys patted Lizzie's arm in a way that meant, Get up. "Fetch me a broom and then off to bed with you. It's been quite a day."

CHAPTER
SIXTEEN

If punking had been paying attention with her eyes, then climbing was paying attention with her whole body.

Olavfur taught her to climb without hurting herself so much. "Sit back like you're in a chair," he said, "but don't rest on the chains. They are there to catch you if you fall, but don't sit on them always. And don't press too hard into the front of the boots, or your toenails will turn purple."

The muscles in her thighs burned. She discovered small muscles at the edges of her knees, muscles at the top of her knees, and they all burned. They ached at night, were stiff in the morning, but loose again after the hike into the woods. Once it was time to work she was ready for the new burn. Her arms and shoulders grew strong from the handling of the rope.

She brought things to Olavfur and took them away. A freshly sharpened saw in exchange for a dull one. A tool to fix a pulley in exchange for a broken pulley part. A full canteen for an empty one. An ax. His lunch.

She had to trust that he was paying attention too and wouldn't drop something on her from his perch as high climber. What prevented injury was cooperation. That was what Pete said. He had learned it in the war. He was right; the men understood. The men shouted and cursed at each other, but the fights blew over. There was no time for sulking. That was what Pete said to Freddie when Freddie was glum about his shoulder, which was healing but not as quickly as he wanted. He had at least a month to rest, said Pete. Otherwise he would re-injure it.

She learned about the men. They'd lived hard lives. Some had children and wives, but most were bachelors. They were orphans too, some said. But no one cared particularly—about telling their stories or listening to hers. She and the men were parts of a machine. This was something she was learning about strength: she wasn't alone. She was strong because of these other people.

Two weeks passed. There was no announcement that anyone was going to Mink Cove. But there were new groceries. One evening after supper, Lizzie saw Gladys replacing empty ketchup bottles on the tables.

Gladys held one bottle under her armpit and hooked another between two fingers. "Can I help you?" she asked Lizzie.

"Did you see any mail, by any chance? That came in with the groceries?" After the last Mink Cove delivery, Gladys had handed letters out in the dining room to the loggers.

Gladys frowned. "What if I did?"

"I'm expecting something from my sister."

"I was going to do mail call tomorrow at breakfast, but I suppose you can have a peek." She cocked her head toward a stack of mail by a box marked RECIPES. "I'll leave you to it."

Gladys left, but Lizzie hesitated. Maybe she didn't want to know. Maybe Boss Veil knew the mail had arrived and was on his way to get it right now. Maybe Wilton was going to stop by on his way to the commissary. But she just had to see—on the off chance.

She looked over each shoulder. Then, as fast as a card dealer, she flipped through the envelopes.

Nothing.

Nothing from her uncle. There were other things for Boss Veil, even something from a mill marked PAYMENT. If Boss Veil had taken his share of the mail, he'd surely have taken that. Which meant there was nothing from her uncle. No ransom. Nothing.

Lizzie fled out the kitchen door, down the path, and through the trees to the small beach with the bone-looking logs. There, the tears came. It wasn't just despair, or fear. It was worse: shame. She had been foolish. Hideously, painfully, terribly foolish. To think that her uncle—someone she'd never met, a man with a family of his own—would want her. She closed her eyes. She felt on the edge of a gaping blackness that wanted to swallow her up. Or maybe it already had.

Crash. There was someone coming down the path. She tensed. There was nowhere to go but where she was. Was it Boss Veil? Had he seen her snooping through the mail? She wiped her nose on her sleeve.

A fluff of white hair. Red.

"I thought I saw you scamper off," he said. "Are you sneaking a smoke?"

She tried to laugh but could only manage a smile.

Red sat next to her and passed her his canteen. She drank from it gratefully. Her mouth felt sticky from the crying. He passed her a clean piece of cloth. She blew her nose into it, hard, a few times, until her nose cleared out. Then he took the canteen back, wetted another piece of cloth, and handed it to her. "For your face."

She wiped the cloth over her face and tasted her salty tears on her lips. She felt as if she had been swimming in the ocean. Wrung out.

She squeezed the water out of the cloth onto the rocks between her knees. "Hey, this is from the kitchen!" she said. "You *are* a thief!"

"Only books and napkins." He showed his palms innocently. Then his face grew serious. "So will you tell me what's going on here?"

Her crying began again. "My uncle didn't send the ransom."

"Hmm," said Red. He lit a cigarette and took his first puff. The sky was gray. Breeze ruffled the water. There'd been talk of a storm coming. Red lowered his hand and tapped the cigarette's end with his index finger. "Tomorrow is our day off, when we go into town. I can send word to your sister from there. If you can sneak me your uncle's address, I'll send him something too. Does your sister have a telephone?"

"No. And she certainly doesn't have any money to pay my ransom."

"She could tell your uncle to pay."

"But he's gone this long without paying. What if he just doesn't care?" She sobbed long and hard. She felt fear, anger, and then grief. Pure, cold grief. Then loneliness. No one wanted her. She looked out at the flat bay. "My father took pills on purpose."

Red was quiet but not for very long.

"It happens more often than we think, doesn't it." Red's voice was matter-of-fact. Not like the adults at the memorial service, who pretended the death was an accident and spoke to her like she was a stupid little girl. And Red said something no one else had said: *more often than we think*. That meant it wasn't just her father. She imagined Red's life. He was old. He had seen many things in many places. And he was saying that her father wasn't so rare. That Lizzie wasn't so rare.

This was a moment to say something true. Someone was waiting to hear her truest, deepest thing. What she felt about Boss Veil and her uncle and her father and everything else. "I just don't know what to do."

Red stamped out his cigarette. "I know you don't. Tomorrow is our day off, but then we'll figure it out. Just don't say anything to the boss."

She nodded. She wouldn't.

"And do you still have more of those *Little Women*? Read about Jo. It's a good night not to be alone."

CHAPTER
SEVENTEEN

The next morning the sky was sunny, but wind whipped along the water. Clouds moved in fast from the north. Waves flapped, as if they were sails themselves.

After breakfast, Lizzie laid her boots and socks on the deck at the front of the boss' house. She didn't need her boots or socks because of the day off. She'd scrubbed the boots' insides with a damp towel and a dab of shampoo. The laces were out and the tongues peeled back. She'd dried the socks overnight by the hearth, but she was laying them out too, in hopes of airing out the smoke smell. Because of the wind, she placed rocks inside the socks, and the boots too, for good measure.

The men hadn't left yet. She could still hear hoots and hollers from the cookhouse. After breakfast, Gladys had set out pots of hot water on the porch, and the men had begun shaving, brushing teeth, and taking off their shirts to wash under their arms. Lizzie had hurried past, worried about what might be taken off next.

Boss Veil was going into town too, to visit a mill. Wilton was in charge of camp while the boss and the men were gone, and he was at the commissary. "I'm selling soap for the first time since the men had their last day off," he said.

Lizzie was rarely on the deck. The view was perfect: dark blue water streaked with green, madrona branches arching over the water, and a bush of yellow leaves she'd never noticed. She planned to spend the day out here, reading. She sat in a wooden armchair with a footrest, and she started a chapter. The girls in the book received a letter from their father, who was away at war. The letter said that he loved them and would be home soon. The girls read it and cried, and their mother told them to be brave while they waited for his return. Lizzie shut the book. The wind was stronger now. The waves were jagged and capped in white. Wind gusted through the trees, and fir needles skittered across the deck.

She heard a noise by the front deck. Something more than the wind. Just as she was about to check the front door, she saw Olavfur coming around onto the far side of the deck.

He didn't bother waving hello. He pointed to her boots and socks, all laid out. "Put them on."

"But it's the day off."

"Not for us. We have a new spar to clear."

Not until she was in the woods, hiking behind Olavfur, did it occur to her that maybe Red had asked him to find her. But there *was* work to be done, it was true. The camp needed a new spar in a new part of the woods because the men had cleared so many logs from the old spot.

Even though it was windy, the forest was warm. Sweat was itchy on her neck. She grew hot and short of breath, but she was glad to be there. She was getting the sadness out. Even though the air was warm, the sky, what little of it she could see through the trees, was dark gray.

"Will it rain?" asked Lizzie.

"Perhaps. But we can stay under the trees."

First Lizzie and Olavfur went to the location of the old spar, where he had a set of special small, medium, and large saws and axes that he used for different stages of the spar-clearing process. They were all dirty.

"You will clean them," said Olavfur.

Lizzie carried two small saws in one hand and an ax in the other, careful not to nick her calves. They walked nearly thirty minutes up a steep hill. While Olavfur climbed the low part of the new spar, she scrubbed the saws and axes with turpentine and steel wool. After a little while, she realized that Olavfur had stopped chopping. She looked to see why. He had climbed out of his harness and maneuvered out onto a branch to investigate something.

Then, the first flicker of lightning. Thunder echoed through the trees. Before that roll of thunder had quieted, there was an explosion inside her ear. A flash. She covered her head with her arms.

Immediately after the light was gone, she heard the flames. They came from high above. They sizzled, then popped, then whooshed. Heat stung her eyes. She looked to the spar. Flames seemed to be leaping down the tree, skipping two or three branches at a time. The flames were only a few branches above Olavfur's head.

He was still out of his harness, out on the limb. He swung down and dangled by two arms, then one. He let go. He took a while to stand up after he hit the ground. Once he did she could tell immediately that he was injured. He gripped his shoulder with one arm. His whole body tilted to the side. When he moved a leg to walk, he cried out in pain, or at least she thought he did. She could barely hear anything above the rush of wind and flames.

A blazing tree limb fell to the ground, not ten feet from where Olavfur was standing. Flames ripped through the underbrush, and the wind, like a demon, whipped the flames up the trunks of two more trees. Hot gusts blew against her face, lifting her hair off her neck. The fire was coming downhill, toward the camp, toward them. Smoke stuffed itself up her nose and down her throat. Her tongue was dry and thick.

Olavfur stumbled toward her. He gestured to her water canteen. They both drank. He pulled a handkerchief from his pocket and soaked it with water. He pressed it over his nose and mouth, then passed it to her to do the same. It did some to help her breathing, but her eyes were stinging as if from the lye soap, but worse. She held the handkerchief back to him, but he shook his head no. She pressed it back to her face.

She forced herself to keep her eyes open as she followed Olavfur down the hill. She skidded on mud and leaves but stayed upright. Finally they reached the main path, but then Olavfur fell. His legs skidded out in front of him, and even though he tried to catch himself with his hands, his head fell against the ground. He lay motionless.

"Help!" she screamed, even though her voice didn't carry over the fire's roars. No one was there to hear anyway. No one at all, anywhere.

She collapsed to her knees and dropped her forehead to her thighs. Her head was light. She wanted to vomit. The sounds were coming from all around, roaring like a family of tigers, stalking her, outnumbering her, ready to tear her body apart. What was it going to feel like to burn? Or suffocate? She sucked air up from the space between her knees, but smoke seemed to be rising from the earth itself.

No one was coming for her. She was exhausted. She wanted it over. She was alive, but only to have one terrible thing happen after another. If she was headed to her death anyway, why not now?

Because of Olavfur. She wasn't going to let another father die.

Try. Take one step.

She pushed herself off the ground. Her head was buzzing, but she managed to stay upright as she stumbled down the path to where Olavfur lay. His shoulder was twisted behind him at a hideous, impossible angle. His eyes were closed, but he was still breathing.

She stuffed the hankercheif into the neck of her blouse, then bent down and pushed her shoulder under the crook of his arm. She tried to lift him. It was no use. He was twice her size, or more. He was straining to speak, and she could barely hear him. "Go!" he said. "Or we will both die."

Then she heard another voice. At first she thought she was imagining it, but then it came again. "Lizzie! Olavfur!"

Freddie. It was Freddie, at her side, his eyes wild, his chest heaving. She stared at him in disbelief, but there was no time to ask him why he was there. Had he come to save them? Please no, she thought. He was going to die too.

Olavfur's eyes fluttered. "Leave me," he coughed.

Lizzie looked around to get her bearings. The wind had slowed and the flames seemed to be moving up the trees rather than racing downhill through the brush. She recognized a large rock, then saw the tree with the cave inside.

The cave. She remembered the story of the man hiding his dog during a fire.

"Let's take him to the tree," she yelled toward Freddie, but her voice was barely audible. Her throat felt as if it were filled with embers. She pointed to the hollowed-out tree.

Freddie gave her a baffled look.

"Like the dog." She met eyes with Freddie, willing him to agree with her. He paused for a moment, then pushed his arm under Olavfur's. She did the same. They were able to lift the top half of his body, enough for Olavfur to stand—but only for a moment. Then he crumpled to the ground again. He pushed them away, shaking his head.

"Drag him!" yelled Freddie.

They pulled him by his arms. His legs skidded limply along the ground. She felt the wind pick up again, gusting at the back of her neck. The fire was coming their way. They dragged Olavfur into the cave. It was larger than she had imagined, spacious enough for him to lie down. The air was cool, even damp. A bubble of what the forest was usually like.

Freddie rotated Olavfur so that his face was pointed away from the cave's opening, rolled him over onto his stomach, and arranged his arms so that they folded around his face. The cave was nearly pitch black, so Lizzie couldn't see his expression. He said nothing. She wondered if he knew the story about the dog.

Outside the cave, the air felt even hotter and thicker than before. Lizzie pressed her bandanna back over her nose and mouth. When she breathed in, she choked on sweat and soot, so she threw the cloth into the bushes.

She looked behind her. The smoke had dried out her eyes so much that the lids felt nearly glued shut, but she could still see bursts of orange. The blaze was uphill, at a distance from them about the length of the cookhouse. The wind was so frenzied with soot and sound, she couldn't tell which way the fire was going.

"Come on!" yelled Freddie.

She ran and ran and ran. She slid on her heels. She hit rocks, jumped over roots, closed her eyes for a few seconds at a time. Please don't fall. Please, just a little longer.

It was only a little longer. She and Freddie made it to the beach. The spaciousness of the bay and the sky made her feel as if she were floating. She and Freddie sat on rocks. They both laid their heads on their knees and tried to catch their breaths. Freddie's eyes were bloodshot, and his whole face was red and swollen. She vomited and tasted ashes.

On the far end of the beach, men were shouting and running. Boats and logs were bobbing and banging in the waves. She closed her eyes. The ground tilted. The wind was still blowing hard, and the sound of the sloshing waves made her feel as if she were slipping into the bay.

A boom of thunder. Then thick, fast, wild rain. Drops pellet-like against her blouse.

Then: men's voices. *Are you hurt? Can you breathe?* Hands propped her up. Water was tipped to her lips. Rain.

She told them Olavfur was in the tree.

Shouting. Men's feet trampling. She was scooped up like a baby and carried. The rain continued. She trembled with cold. Then came sleep.

CHAPTER EIGHTEEN

Yellow sunlight came through an awning. The air smelled of hot plants.

Lizzie woke up on the cookhouse porch. She was draped in a blanket. Four cookhouse chairs were pushed together in a row to make a bed. Freddie was sitting on his own makeshift bed, sipping water from a tin mug. Gladys was peeling potatoes, and at her feet was a crate of turnips with long leafy fronds wilting in the heat.

"You're awake," noticed Gladys, as brusque as ever.

Freddie nodded and gave Lizzie a tired smile. His eyes were bloodshot, and his shirt was streaked with soot.

"Drink this," instructed Gladys. She put down a potato and passed a mug of water to Lizzie, who gulped it down, then motioned for more, which Gladys provided from a pitcher next to her. The smell of charred wood clogged the air.

"Where is the fire?" asked Lizzie. Her voice was hoarse. Her ears were ringing. She felt the vibrations of branches falling. She felt heat everywhere on her skin. Her body was shaking. "Do we need to leave?"

"No," said Gladys. She put her hand on Lizzie's knee. She looked her in the eye and waited for Lizzie to look back at her. "It rained. The fire is over."

"All of it?"

"Yes. And Olavfur is alive. They carried him out of that tree, barely breathing, but he survived. They're taking him to the hospital in Vancouver now because he broke his leg. What were you thinking, putting him in a tree?"

Lizzie struggled to answer. She thought mainly of the dog, but then remembered how heavy Olavfur had been. She remembered his telling her to leave him. She remembered the hot air rising from the ground, the feeling of the flames chasing them down the hill.

"Are you sure?" Lizzie asked. "Are you sure the fire is over?"

"Yes." Gladys gave Lizzie's knee a pat.

"You've been asleep for the whole afternoon," said Freddie. His voice was raspy. His face was pink, as if he had a terrible sunburn. Her own skin felt hot and tender.

Gladys handed her and Freddie their own peelers and bucket and scooted the sack of potatoes so they could all three reach it.

Pete came jogging up the path to the porch. "Lizzie! Freddie! You're awake. Last I saw you, you were passed out. I'm glad you got some rest. May I take a look at you?"

Lizzie nodded. He pressed down her tongue with a wooden depressor and peered down her throat. "Even without a lamp I can tell you're swollen. You inhaled a lot of smoke. But you'll heal up in a couple of days." He removed the depressor and studied her admiringly. "Really. I cannot believe you made it out. Whose idea was it to put Olavfur in the tree? It was smart. He had a good pocket of oxygen in there, protected from the fire."

"It was her idea," said Freddie. "I just helped drag him."

Lizzie looked to Freddie. "Why were you in the woods, anyway?"

"I was looking for you and Olavfur so that I could help with the saws. My shoulder's feeling better. I thought I might start doing some climbing again." Freddie looked sheepish, seeing as how no one was going to be doing any climbing any time soon.

Pete patted Freddie's back. "I'm glad you didn't re-injure yourself hauling around a grown man."

Lizzie wanted to lie down in her bed in Boss Veil's loft. She was so tired, and she didn't want all this noise and light. But she didn't want to go back to Boss Veil's house. She didn't want to be alone. The sounds and smells of the fire would haunt her. It all still felt so close.

"May I sleep with you tonight?" she asked Gladys.

Gladys stopped her peeling. "Good heavens. Of course."

After dinner, when night had fallen and Lizzie wanted to change out of her sooty clothes and into her nightgown, she went to the boss' house to retrieve her things.

Wilton answered the door. Weariness marked his face. His black hair hung messily over his black brows. He opened the door but said nothing. Inside, the boss sat in front of the fireplace. Seeing the flames, even small ones contained by the stone hearth and a metal screen, Lizzie wanted to run back down the porch.

"Who's there?" barked the boss. He raised himself, leaning heavily on the armrest of the chair. His balance was unsteady. His droopy-lidded eyes took a few moments to know what they were looking at. "If it isn't the orphan," he said. On the coffee table, an empty glass glittered in the firelight.

"I'm here to get my bag," said Lizzie.

"You," said the boss. "*You*. I didn't have any trouble at this camp until you arrived. But now look at this place. It nearly burned to the ground. Do you know how much money we lost? Do you *know*? More than an acre of old growth. A thousand times the price of *you*." He nearly spat out those last words. He swayed and gripped the arm of the chair to steady himself.

Disgusting, she thought. To blame a fire on her! "Are you joking?" she asked. She took a step toward him and raised her voice. "The fire wasn't my fault. It was lightning." She gestured upward, toward the ceiling, and thought of what Red would say. "It was an act of an angry god! And I saved someone. I saved Olavfur. Didn't you know that?"

"You put him in a tree! That's not saving someone."

"Well, he survived."

194

"'He survived,'" mocked the boss in a girlish voice. "Get out of my sight." He thrust his body again, trying to step forward, but his legs wobbled under him. He tumbled into his chair. A gulping, crying sound came from him.

Lizzie's indignation softened into fear, then disgust, then pity. A grown man, weeping like a child.

Wilton ignored the boss' sobs. "Well, off with you," he said to Lizzie. "Get your things."

Upstairs, Lizzie hastily took her clothes from the open shelves where she'd folded them and pressed them into her bag. Her tin suit was filthy, but she packed it alongside her clothes anyway. Her bag was nearly too full to latch shut, but she managed it. Her fingers lingered on the latch, and she surveyed her room. Her little loft. To her surprise, she was sad to go. It had been a place of her own. Kind of. She thought of her stolen money and her rummaged-through clothes. No, it had never been hers. It was time to go.

Downstairs, the boss was still on the floor. Wilton asked, "Do you need help carrying your things?"

"No, thank you," she said.

"Well, don't forget this. You left it on the deck." He handed her *Little Women*.

"Thank you," she said. "Goodnight."

Lizzie walked back through the woods toward the cookhouse. Halfway there, she heard a voice.

"Hey there, Miss Lizzie." It was Red. He was up on his knoll, perched on his coffin, puffing the day's last cigarette. "Come up here."

She walked up the knoll. Although the rain had stopped several hours before, the soil was damp. Her footsteps were quiet on the path.

Red looked over Lizzie's shoulder and gestured. "You too."

It was Freddie, walking with a deck of cards. "I'm headed to poker."

"You can spare a minute," said Red.

Freddie joined them on the knoll, and Red pulled back the lid of his coffin. He fiddled with something inside. "There are matches and a lantern there," he said, tilting his head to a nearby rock. Lizzie lit the lantern and flooded the coffin with light. She and Freddie looked on as Red, with a screwdriver, pried a board away from the bottom of the coffin. She squinted at shadows. There, like a second floor, was a layer of dark bricks. Something shiny glinted in the bounce of the lamplight. Silver. They were silver bricks.

"Where did all this come from?" asked Lizzie.

"Back during the '80s, my railroad job took me out to Colorado, which was just a territory back then. I worked at a silver mine and developed an engine for a little machine similar to a donkey and started a little company. It was easier to sell that engine than mine the silver, that's for sure, and so I made this little fortune in only a few years. Silver is hard to carry around, but hard to steal too. And people always steal the gold first."

Freddie let out a long whistle. "Well, I'll be."

Red continued. "Two weeks ago on my day in the city, I learned about a little patch of woods that's come up for sale. Fifty acres out by Urchin Bay. Then I thought, what the hell?"

Freddie looked at him. "You bought it? You want to set up your own camp? When?"

"Now! I'm old! I'd need help, of course. I've already asked Olavfur, Pete, and Wally, and I'm sure I can get some other fellas. And now I'm asking you."

"Us?" Freddie was even more incredulous now.

Red nodded. "Until Olavfur is back in action, Pete can clear the first spar, and you two can help. And be on fire patrol."

"I'm in!" exclaimed Freddie.

Red looked to Lizzie. "Miss Parker?"

Lizzie had never heard of Urchin Bay. She couldn't imagine setting up a camp from scratch. She couldn't imagine setting a foot back in the woods after today. All she wanted was to lie down. "You look like you're going to be sick," said Freddie. "I'll walk you to the cookhouse."

"Sleep well, my girl," said Red. He put the board back over the silver, snuffed out his lantern, and climbed inside his coffin.

Lizzie and Freddie walked slowly in the peace of the forest. The men in the cabins were quieter than normal. A mourning feeling, even though no one had died. Had it really been just that morning that she and Freddie had outrun a fire? A lifetime had passed. Two lifetimes had passed since Freddie had hopped out of the truck and passed her a sack of flour. Now they knew each other. Better than boyfriend-girlfriend. Friends.

They arrived at the cookhouse porch and paused. "It was smart," said Freddie. "What you did with Olavfur."

"I couldn't have done it without you."

He reached out with one hand and gently touched her hand. For a moment she wondered if he would kiss her, but then he dropped his hand away. He didn't say anything. He turned and walked toward the cabins. She remained there, listening to the rocks and branches move with his footsteps, until she could no longer hear him. Her heart ached. It felt as full and wide as the bay itself.

Lizzie slept soundly on the pallet Gladys had arranged for her on the floor of her room. A dressing screen separated her from Gladys's bed and the morning light, and so she was still sleeping when she heard a knock on the bedroom door.

Lizzie folded back the screen.

"Is that you?" she asked, expecting Gladys.

"It's Wilton."

Lizzie grabbed the sheet from the bed and draped it around herself like a cloak to hide her nightgown. She opened the door, and Wilton entered carrying a tray with food and coffee. He set it on the upholstered stool where she had sat weeks ago for her haircut. He looked at her with more intensity than she had ever seen from him. His glance darted to the door and then back to her.

"Eat quickly," he said. "And then gather your things. You'll be leaving in an hour to go to Vancouver. Your uncle will be waiting for you."

"My *uncle*? What are you talking about?"

"I saw him last night at the hospital. I had gone with Olavfur in the morning, and by the end of the day your uncle had heard the story about the fire. Word had traveled fast among the mill workers and investors that a little girl at Dark Water Bay had put a man in a tree and saved him. And your uncle put it together that it must be you. So, he's sent for you."

"Sent for me?"

"He says he'll meet you at the dock this afternoon, and you can stay with him for the rest of the summer."

Lizzie struggled to understand. Her uncle, after all this time! "But what about Boss Veil? Will he let me go?"

"He doesn't know. He's in the woods, surveying the fire damage. I told him he needed to do that right away for the insurance, and that I'd look after you."

Wilton looked at her with urgency. She thought about what he'd said. He'd told the boss to go far into the woods by himself. Wilton was helping her. She thought of his foot. *The other men like me have no place to go.* He was trapped, but Lizzie could leave.

"You really think my uncle will be there?"

"I talked with him myself. And if he's not, one of the men will help you get to the train station. Here." Wilton passed her ten dollars. "Payment for four weeks of good work."

CHAPTER NINETEEN

Late that afternoon, the ferry cut its engines and drifted into its dock at Vancouver. Lizzie stood on the boat's top deck and looked out at the rows of other ships. Sailboats were at full sail. Clouds of smoke billowed from the ferries. Tugboats hauled pyramids of cut logs, maybe even some from Dark Water Bay.

She had left that morning with men who were going into the city for their days off. She knew none of them well. Because they had to leave early to catch the steamship—by way of the motorboat and truck—her good-byes had been mercifully brief. Little more than a nod to Wilton, and business-like handshakes with Gladys and Wally. Freddie was back to his taciturn self, saying simply, "Good-bye." Pete told her to keep drinking plenty of water for her throat.

Red said, "If you change your mind about Urchin Bay, find Olavfur in the hospital, and I'll pick you two up. We're leaving tomorrow at noon."

"In your broken boat?" she teased.

"She's a thing of beauty," he winked.

Now, in the Vancouver harbor, ropes creaked as men tied the ship into its moorings. Passengers began walking down the gangway onto the dock. Lizzie drew in her breath. She looked at herself as she imagined her uncle would see her. Although she was wearing her cleanest dress, it was still wrinkled and smelled of smoke and sawdust. Stockings long gone, her legs were bare. Mosquito bites, scratches, and bruises covered her skin. Her face felt hot, as if she had a sunburn but even more uncomfortable.

She was in no rush to find her uncle. She knew his house couldn't be worse than Dark Water Bay had been, yet she couldn't shake a melancholy feeling. He hadn't paid her ransom. Why did he want her now? Part of Lizzie wanted to go to Seattle and avoid him altogether. Her coin purse with Wilton's ten dollars— no, *her* ten dollars—was tucked inside her suitcase. She could go straight from the dock to the train station.

But then she imagined Esther meeting her in Seattle. Her face would be full of disappointment. She would ask, "Where's the hundred dollars? What am I to do with the boarders?" Even though Lizzie would explain about Boss Veil and the ransom, it would all sound like a tall tale. The only person who'd want to understand the story would be Mary. And staying in Seattle with Mary meant earning a hundred dollars, and to do that she'd have to work for her uncle.

She followed the other passengers onto the dock. Even in the bustle of people, she spotted her uncle easily. Although he wasn't in wedding clothes, he looked nearly identical to his photo: tall, with a tidy black beard and long, straight nose.

"Elizabeth?" he called out.

"Uncle Andrew?"

He rushed to her and embraced her. He smelled of spicy soap. His beard was soft. He let her go and then took her suitcase. He looked at her with genuine-seeming concern. Compared to the loggers' skin, his looked as pale and smooth as a child's. His eyes were hazel.

"Here, let's sit." He found them a bench. He put his hand on her knee, then moved it back to his own. His dress pants were black and pressed with a careful center seam.

"I am so sorry," he said. "I didn't know you were at camp. I didn't get the letters from Mr. Veil until just today. After I left camp in May, my investment firm moved to a new office, and we didn't give Boss Veil the new address. He was such a despicable man and had been harassing me to reconsider an investment. I decided it'd be better never to hear from him again. I'm sure it won't surprise you to know, but he is a scoundrel of a businessman. A world-class cheat. Within a week at camp, I saw him sending rotting logs to a mill and mismarking wood and selling it as a higher grade. He wasn't even ashamed. I decided to withdraw my investment right then. And besides, your Aunt Louise hated the woods."

Lizzie thought of all those rafts of logs and how Boss Veil always oversaw operations at the beach. He was shipping rotten wood and passing off one kind for another. Wilton was the scheme's loyal bookkeeper.

Her uncle continued. "Once I heard the news about a girl saving a man in a fire, I couldn't help but wonder whether it was you. How many girls are there at logging camps? And then I went back to the old offices and found Veil's terrible ransom notes . . ." Her uncle's voice wavered. He looked at his lap. "I should've made sure that Esther had received my letter telling you not to come," said her uncle. "I should've tried harder. Especially after all that happened with your father—"

"Please," she stopped him. She didn't want to talk about her father. "Have you telephoned Esther?"

"No," he said. "I wanted to locate you first. Just as soon as I found out. But we should phone her. She must be worried sick!"

"I don't think so. The boss faked telegrams to let her know that I was there and all right. He pretended they were from you."

"Oh, what a terrible man." Her uncle grimaced, as if he'd tasted spoiled food. "I feel so wretched about all of this. Believe me when I say that I do. Had I known what would happen—"

"It's all right," said Lizzie, although she wasn't sure it was. He hadn't kidnapped her, but he hadn't made sure that she didn't go to the camp. She didn't want to talk about it. She wanted him to stop talking. The world felt noisy and crowded, and she didn't want to hear his voice. The sights and sounds and smells around her were making her feel dizzy and strange. "It's all right," she repeated. "I'm just tired."

"Well, then let's get you home," he said. "Follow me to the car." He sounded relieved to finish the conversation. He picked up her suitcase, and she accompanied him down the busy sidewalk. Everything seemed so modern. Sidewalks, pavement, streetlamps. Women wearing dresses and lipstick. Well-dressed children licking ice cream cones.

Her uncle's black Model T was so clean, it gleamed. The windshield sparkled as if just washed. Lizzie remembered meeting Freddie and Red at the dusty truck over a month ago. How far she and her little suitcase had traveled. The car smelled of exhaust and new leather and some kind of cleaning product.

"Music?" asked her uncle as he turned the key in the ignition.

"Sure," she said, and he twisted a knob. Scratchy jazz sounded as if it were coming from a great distance, and even though the volume was low, the sound was too loud. Lizzie and her uncle drove without speaking over the racket of the music and the motor. They left the bustle of the harbor and entered a part of town organized with tall clapboard houses. Ornate carvings topped windows. Leafy trees shadowed wraparound porches. Children played with balls on sidewalks.

Her uncle parked in front of a large white house with a lush green lawn and purple rhododendrons. The window trims were black, and the door—a double one, with shining brass fixtures—was red. Before her uncle had even turned his key in the lock, someone opened the door.

"Sir?" At first Lizzie wondered if it were Aunt Louise, but it was a young woman, only slightly older than Lizzie herself, dressed in a gray uniform with a white hat and white apron. "Good evening," said the girl, and curtseyed slightly as she opened the door.

"Elizabeth," said her uncle, "this is Rose. Rose, meet my niece Elizabeth."

The girl, Rose, nodded silently and then fixed her gaze on the floor. Lizzie looked around her new surroundings. The foyer was high-ceilinged with a grand curved staircase. A tall tropical-looking tree stood in a large blue porcelain pot. The floors were polished wood. Lizzie chuckled to herself, imagining loggers charging across them in their caulk boots.

"Hello, my dear! We finally meet."

It was her Aunt Louise, descending down the stairs. She wore a navy drop-waist dress with a white collar and sash, everything silky and expensive, and low heels with a buckle across the ankle. Her dark hair was parted to the side and curled into a bun at the nape of her neck. Sapphires twinkled on her ears. She offered an airy kiss to Lizzie's right cheek. She smelled of perfume and talc.

"Nice to meet you," said Lizzie. "Thank you for, um, having me."

"We are just so sorry about the misunderstanding," Louise said. Her voice was warm and sophisticated.

Lizzie couldn't tell whether she was offering kindness or politeness. "Wait, is that smoke I smell?" she asked, sniffing the air.

"Louise. She's just been in a fire," reminded her uncle.

"That's right, you poor dear," said her aunt. "Well, you will have a bath right away. And I say we toss those clothes in the rubbish bin and shop for some new ones tomorrow. Rose, draw Miss Parker a bath. A quite deep one. And take up her bag, and find her some clean clothes."

Rose murmured, "Yes ma'am," and hurried up the stairs with Lizzie's suitcase.

On an entryway table, next to a vase of yellow tulips, sat a polished wooden telephone with a brass mouthpiece. Lizzie had never seen a telephone indoors before.

Her uncle must have caught her staring, because he asked, "Would you like to make a call?"

"No, thank you," she said. "I want to talk to Esther, but she doesn't have a telephone. I can telegraph her."

Just then, two young boys came running into the foyer. They each wore vests, short pants, knee socks, and polished loafers. Their hair was neatly combed, and they looked nearly the same except one was taller.

"Introduce yourselves," prompted Aunt Louise.

"I'm Theodore," announced the taller boy. "I'm ten."

"And I'm Frank," said the shorter one. "I'm seven."

"Hello. I'm Lizzie. I'm very pleased to meet you."

"She's going to be your governess," said Uncle Andrew.

"But we already have a governess," said Theodore, with a note of having been betrayed.

"Hush, boys." Her aunt looked to Lizzie, with an eye roll in Theodore's direction. "Never mind him. We did hire another governess, but we can still find something to do with you."

Lizzie nodded, but her heart sank. She didn't want something "found" for her. She knew what that meant: we don't want you, or need you, which maybe meant the same thing. She didn't want to stand with this family in the foyer for another moment. "Should I go take my bath?" she asked.

"Of course!" said Aunt Louise. Your bedroom is the first door on the left."

Lizzie's room had a tidy bed with a yellow bedspread and a white canopy. Yellow hummingbirds patterned the wallpaper. A soft white carpet was underfoot. A small desk stood in the corner, and on it was a white lamp with a white shade. Under it waited a box of fancy-looking paper with matching envelopes, and a pen and jar of ink. She lifted the pen but didn't ink it. Idly, she ran the sharp metal tip over a sheet of paper, pretend-writing as if she were a child. She hadn't written anything in an entire month. Did she have anything to say? To whom? She didn't have Mary's vacation address any longer. And Esther . . . it all seemed too much to communicate in a letter. What she wanted to do, to her surprise, was to draw a diagram of how the spar tree worked, with all the pulleys and ropes, so that one day she wouldn't forget. So that she could see it again now.

There was a little rap on the door.

"Come in," said Lizzie, half expecting Wilton.

It was Rose. "May I come in?"

"Of course."

The maid scuttled in without another word and spread a peachy-pink cotton dress on the bed. She smoothed out the pristine white collar. "This is the Missus's, but it'll do until you have something of your own." Without meeting Lizzie's eyes, Rose laid out stockings, underwear, and a camisole also. Lizzie flushed. Were her own underthings not good enough? Had her aunt decided they must be as dirty as the rest of her, and she didn't want them touching her dress?

Lizzie tried to conceal her embarrassment. "Thank you," she said.

"Of course, Miss. Your bath is just down the hall." Rose nodded in that direction and left Lizzie by herself.

The bathroom had a tall window draped in white lace. Black-and-white tile covered the floor. As Lizzie undressed, she noticed how suntanned her legs and arms had become while the rest of her remained pale. She hadn't once been fully naked since she'd arrived at camp; she'd only washed with the cloth from the basin. Standing in the bathroom now, she clutched herself and locked the door in case her boisterous cousins came barging in or Rose wanted to wait on her.

In the bath, so much dirt and ash floated off Lizzie that the water turned gray almost instantly. She had to drain the water and refill the bath, and even then the water turned gray again. The water had grown cold by the time she finished scrubbing her fingernails and toenails.

Be happy, she told herself. You are safe. There are no boat sheds or ransom notes or fires. You are safe. Lucky.

There was another knock on the door, then Rose's quiet voice. "It's nearly time for dinner, Miss."

"Of course," said Lizzie, rushing to step out of the bath. "I'll be right down."

Quickly Lizzie dried off and dressed in Aunt Louise's underclothes and dress, which were all too big. The stockings, however, felt tight and terrible. The tops dug into her thighs, and her garter belt felt like a vise around her waist. A tortoiseshell comb waited on a panel of lace in front of a mirror. Lizzie combed her wet hair and looked at herself, remembering the haircut in Gladys's room. What Gladys would think of all this. Gladys, who spent her winters urinating on a dock to keep otters away.

A fluttering sound came from the window. Leaves against glass. Lizzie went to the window and opened it. Outside the window, a grand leafy tree—an oak? a maple?—curved its branches around the house. Lizzie cracked open her window, reached out, and touched a leaf. Surrounded by fir trees for so long, she was charmed by how silky and flat the leaf was. The branches were thick and knotted, and they stretched out nearly parallel to the ground. A perfect climbing tree.

Not now. Time for dinner.

In the dining room, Aunt Louise and the boys were already seated. Rose stood in the corner but didn't make eye contact. Uncle Andrew pulled out a chair for Lizzie. "Welcome, distinguished guest," he said, in a voice intended to be funny, but no one laughed. Lizzie felt embarrassed by her wet hair; she felt like a dog that had been swimming and had run ashore. No one made any comment. She hoped that she smelled less of smoke.

Dinner was asparagus and thin fillets of beef. Lizzie made a great effort to remember her manners. Her silverware worked gently against the plate, and she chewed quietly and slowly. Her throat was still sore every time she swallowed.

"Your hair is crooked," announced the younger boy, out of the blue. He was staring at Lizzie.

"Frank!" chided her uncle.

"That's all right," said Lizzie. "It wasn't cut at a real hair parlor. A cook named Gladys cut it because I'd gotten pitch in it while I was climbing a tree."

"I know how to climb trees," boasted the cousin.

"Well, these were very tall trees. Taller than your house, or even the buildings downtown."

"You remember, Frankie," prompted her aunt. "From the camp. You didn't do any climbing. All you learned how to do was swear from those filthy men."

"I could've climbed those if you'd let me, mother," whined the boy. "I could've made it to the top."

"It's harder than it looks," said Lizzie. She worried that she was being impertinent, but she couldn't stop herself. If he'd been boasting at a table in the Dark Water Bay cookhouse, no one would've let him get away with bragging. "You have to use a harness and all sorts of ropes and special boots with nails sticking out of them. I worked as the assistant to the high climber, who is the man who climbs to the very tops of trees."

Her uncle set down the knife he was using to cut his meat. "You didn't!" he said, looking at her in disbelief.

"I did," she said. "I started as a whistle punk, but then my friend Freddie hurt his arm—"

"How dreadful," shuddered Aunt Louise. "That work isn't for girls. Those men are all terrible. It's a wonder you didn't fall to your death! I can't stand even to hear about it."

Lizzie looked down at her plate. She wanted to say the work was for girls, and she hadn't fallen to her death, and the men weren't all terrible. But she said nothing. Her aunt didn't want to hear anything else. This feeling—this silence—was something she knew. It was how she'd felt at her father's memorial service, at school when her classmates whispered about her because her father had died, at Esther's house when she had burned the pork chops. It was the feeling of pretending nothing was wrong even when everything was.

Aunt Louise filled the silence. "I'll take you to my hairdresser tomorrow, dear. We'll get your hair evened out, and then it will all grow back eventually. Don't worry."

Lizzie looked at her aunt's long, shiny hair wrapped into a bun. She felt her cheeks burn. She looked at her plate and pushed the beef in a circle.

"I'm afraid I've got to go lie down. I'm still tired from the fire."

"Very well," said her aunt. "Tomorrow morning I must supervise Frankie's handwriting lesson, but then in the afternoon, you and I shall go shopping."

Upstairs, Lizzie brushed her teeth, changed into her nightgown, and slipped into bed. Her nightgown seemed so dingy against the clean white sheets that she took it off and changed back into Aunt Louise's underwear. But no, she didn't want to sleep in someone else's underwear. She put the nightgown back on. She was still uncomfortable. There was too much noise and light. Automobiles rumbled past. A streetlamp glowed, but the tree and pale curtains did little to block it out. Her heart beat its wings inside her chest so fast that she wondered if she'd be able to sleep at all.

She was grateful her uncle had rescued her. She was grateful that he and Aunt Louise had taken her into this beautiful house. She was grateful not to be held for ransom anymore. Of course she was; part of her wanted to weep with relief. But another, larger part of her didn't feel relief at all. She was still trapped.

She awoke at five o'clock. Time to go to the cookhouse and eat enough sausage to last her till lunch. Her stomach rumbled, and her throat stung.

The bathroom had no cup for water. She listened for noises from downstairs. Nothing. She could try the kitchen. She tiptoed down the grand staircase, careful to walk on the sides of the stairs closest to the banister to avoid creaks. She made it to the kitchen with barely a sound, but it didn't matter. Aunt Louise was already awake. She sat, sipping from a coffee cup, at a small marble table. Her long hair was in a thick braid draped over one shoulder. She wore a white dressing gown. Without makeup, her face looked softer, and less beautiful.

"Lizzie," she said. "What are you doing up?"

"I'm on camp time, I suppose."

"You most certainly are." Aunt Louise looked surprised and irritated, but also resigned. A mother who was accustomed to children waking her up. But not someone else's child.

"Rose hasn't cooked breakfast yet, but there is coffee, if you like. Cups are in the cabinet over the stove."

As Lizzie reached for the cabinet, her aunt said, "Well, well. Any other habits you picked up from the men? Would you like a little snoose too?"

Lizzie **poured** herself a cup, but she couldn't bring herself to sip from it. She stood against the counter and let the delicate cup rattle in its saucer.

"Sit," said Aunt Louise.

Lizzie did, and felt nervous that the morning light through the doors to the balcony were shining through her nightgown. She crossed her arms high over her chest.

Her aunt set down her own coffee and studied Lizzie. "Since the boys don't need a governess," she said, "we'll have to find something else to do with you. That's what I was awake here thinking about. My friend Eve has a daughter your age, and you could pal around. I imagine she is already scheduled for her own lessons, but you could still be acquainted. Maybe you could play tennis, or sail. It'd only be how long until you return home?"

"My school begins in September, so that is one month away." Or a geological age, thought Lizzie. She wanted nothing less than to pal around with a strange girl.

"Well, that is not so very long," said her aunt with a pinched smile. "What do you think? Tennis or sailing, or both?"

"What about a job?" asked Lizzie.

"A job?" Now it was her aunt's turn to look embarrassed. "Of course! You need the wages. That was the whole point of your summer adventure. Your uncle and I can just write you a check. I mean, you were supposed to be the boys' governess, so we can pay you that. How much is it?"

Lizzie couldn't say a hundred. It felt like too much to ask for, but also too little to confess that would make a difference to her and Esther and Thomas. She'd never felt poorer in her life. Not even at the ferry dock with Freddie and Red when she'd had only coins in her pocket. "No," stammered Lizzie. "I can't take your money if I'm not doing any work."

Just then Rose came in. She was tying her apron around her waist, and if she were surprised to see Aunt Louise and Lizzie, she said nothing except, "Good morning. Shall I start breakfast?"

"Yes, please. Lizzie? A fried egg?"

Or three, thought Lizzie, but she only said, "Yes, please. Thank you, Rose."

Rose proceeded to fetch the eggs from the ice box, and although Louise turned her attention away from the girl, she became more formal in her presence. "We can discuss this more tonight," said Aunt Louise, in a clipped voice. "Once I have a chance to speak to your uncle."

Aunt Louise didn't want to talk about money in front of the servant.

Lizzie ate her egg as hastily as possible without seeming unmannerly, she hoped. Aunt Louise flipped through the newspaper. Rose bustled at the counter and started a skillet of bacon. "For the boys," said Aunt Louise. "I try to watch my figure." She offered none to Lizzie, which was just as well because she wanted to escape the kitchen as soon as possible.

In the foyer, she ran into her cousins. They were charging down the stairs, the older one sliding his hand down the banister and making chugging sounds as if his hand were a train on a track. "Choo choo! Look out!" He ran to the bottom step, took his hand off the banister, and flashed his palm toward Lizzie's face as if his hand were exploding. "Pow! Got you!"

"Got me? With a train?" asked Lizzie, unable to hide her annoyance.

Her cousin appeared undeterred by her logic. "Well, you don't stink as much as yesterday," he said, "but your hair's still crooked."

He snickered and elbowed the littler one, who snickered also. Lizzie stopped herself from touching her hair. She looked at the boys' pressed white collars, pleated short pants, and shoes shined by a servant. They were the ones who looked silly.

"Forget you," she said. She walked quickly past her cousins, and they continued their train game toward the kitchen. *Pow! Crash!* She thought of Freddie. He'd give them swats to the head and tell them to buzz off. Oh, Freddie. Her heart squeezed, and she felt tears gather.

She shut the door to her room. On the dresser, the clock said it wasn't even seven. Seven o'clock in the morning on her first day. She hadn't been here twenty-four hours. How could she last a month? "Pal around" with a stranger? Play tennis? She had never set foot on a court, let alone held a racquet.

Lizzie flopped herself back on the bed and stared at the ceiling. She could ask her uncle for the money and go home tomorrow, but if she went back to Seattle, she'd have a whole month to fill there too. Surely the job at the milliner's was taken. She would end up taking care of Robert, changing diapers, and wiping up messes while Esther complained that she wasn't doing anything right.

Father, what should I do?

She imagined him setting down *Popular Mechanics* and giving her a calm, thoughtful look. She imagined the twinkle in his eye he'd had before it had gone dark with sorrow.

Liz, I hear you've gotten good at climbing trees.

She walked across the bedroom and opened the window by the large tree. The cool morning air smelled of pavement and dew. She reached out and was able to touch the scratchy trunk with her fingertips. She wanted to climb. She wanted to sharpen saws and throw ropes. Her legs and arms were meant to burn under heavy weights, her brow was supposed to drip with sweat, and her chest was meant to heave for air. She was alive. She was strong.

And she wasn't alone. Red had said to meet him at noon at the hospital, and they would go together to the new camp.

Using the stationery from the little desk, Lizzie wrote a letter to Esther. *I'm all right. I will be back home in time for school. I have a job that no one else can do.*

She folded the note and lay it on her pillow. She changed into her pantaloons and tin pants, the waist of which she tightened with her tattered sash. Her socks and caulk boots smelled of soot and filth as she tugged and cinched them around her feet.

She packed her suitcase, double-checked the latch, and threw it out the window. It landed with a loud thud but didn't spring open. She had to follow quickly in case someone had heard the noise.

Her legs moved nimbly out the window. Her boots dug into the bark. Her legs and hands found places to hang on. She trusted herself and the force that was pulling her back to the woods.